All the best,
Karen Charles

FATEFUL CONNECTIONS

KAREN CHARLES

© 2023 Karen Charles

All rights reserved. No part of this publication may be reproduced, distributed, or transmitted in any form or by any means, including photocopying, recording, or other electronic or mechanical methods, without the prior written permission of the publisher, except in the case of brief quotations embodied in critical reviews and certain other non-commercial uses permitted by copyright law.

Print ISBN: 978-1-66789-604-5
eBook ISBN: 978-1-66789-605-2

Dedicated to Sandy, my good friend, my fellow teacher, and my inspiration.

TABLE OF CONTENTS

PART ONE: DANGEROUS INTERSECTIONS   1

Chapter One 3

Chapter Two 6

Chapter Three 9

Chapter Four 11

Chapter Five 15

Chapter Six 19

Chapter Seven 21

Chapter Eight 23

Chapter Nine 26

Chapter Ten 28

Chapter Eleven 30

Chapter Twelve – One Year Later 33

PART TWO: DANGEROUS CONNECTIONS   35

Chapter Thirteen 37

Chapter Fourteen 40

Chapter Fifteen 43

Chapter Sixteen 47

Chapter Seventeen 51

Chapter Eighteen 54

Chapter Nineteen 57

Chapter Twenty 61

Chapter Twenty-One 65

Chapter Twenty-Two *68*

Chapter Twenty-Three *70*

Chapter Twenty-Four *74*

Chapter Twenty-Five *78*

Chapter Twenty-Six *82*

Chapter Twenty-Seven *86*

Chapter Twenty-Eight *89*

PART ONE:

DANGEROUS INTERSECTIONS

CHAPTER ONE

EVERYONE WAS STUNNED. THE CONFERENCE room was hushed except for a gasp here and there. The gigantic screen above the stage had lit up with the news that the North Tower of the New York World Trade Center had been impaled by a massive jet liner. Fire was pouring from the eightieth-story windows. Was this a terrible accident? Eyes were glued to the report as first responders rushed to the horrific scene.

A round-table group of four looked at each other in disbelief. They watched, mesmerized by the enormity of the implications. Only eighteen minutes had gone by when a second Boeing 767 appeared, turning sharply toward the World Trade Center, and slicing into the seventy-fifth through the eighty-fifth floors of the South Tower. The massive explosion rained down burning debris. These were not accidents! America was under attack.

Planned closing conference speeches were immediately canceled. Speakers and participants were all dismissed. Henry, the group's leader, suggested they all meet in the hotel bar. In quick agreement, they found a table where they could continue to watch the news. No one wanted to hang out in his room alone. They somberly ordered drinks as they listened to President Bush call the events a terrorist attack on our country. Six minutes later, Flight

77 crashed into the western façade of the Pentagon. At 9:37 in the morning, the building would be full of military and civilian personnel.

The traumatized conference group sipped their drinks in shock. The sudden collapse of the South Tower was too much to take in for Harper. Her big, brown eyes filled with tears as she tightly hugged herself. Another hour went by before they heard of another plane crashing into a field in Somerset County, Pennsylvania.

Ethan, sensing how upset everyone was feeling, suggested they head up to his suite. The Bell Harbor International Conference Center on the waterfront in Seattle offered spacious suites where they could continue to watch the news. Rain ran in rivulets down his expansive windows, obscuring his waterfront view. No one was interested in the view anyway. Without asking anyone what they wanted, he ordered lunch and drinks for all.

Owen plopped down in the closest easy chair to the TV. President Bush was announcing that U.S. Navy destroyers had been dispatched to New York and Washington, DC.

"Owen, you have a brother living in New York, don't you?" asked Henry.

"I do," Owen answered, with a little catch in his voice. "He shouldn't have any reason to be near the Trade Center. I'll give him a call."

Owen called, leaving a message to return his call as soon as possible.

The foursome munched their way through the afternoon, rarely taking their eyes off the dreadful news. Owen had just stepped out onto the covered balcony for a breath of fresh air when he heard a scream. He rushed back into the sitting room. Harper had her hand over her mouth, sobbing softly. Henry had his strong arm around her shoulders trying to comfort her. The second tower had collapsed after burning for hours. The lower floors had been evacuated. The unspeakable terror seemed nonstop.

President Bush was making another announcement. The Federal Aviation Administration had issued the first national ground stop in US history, prohibiting departures for all civilian aircraft. After the third hijacked plane struck the Pentagon, all aircraft were ordered to land at the nearest airport. Three and a half hours after the first plane hit, all US airspace was clear.

Suddenly, Ethan, who had been unusually quiet, jumped to his feet. "Our flights!" he yelled. "We don't have any way to get home!"

The room was silent. "Maybe we could rent a car," Harper suggested.

Henry sprang into action, calling every car rental agency in Seattle. Nothing was available. Dismayed, he sank into his chair. "What are we going to do now?"

After thoughtful silence, Owen spoke up. "I have a friend over on Yesler Way who repossesses cars. Maybe he might have an idea what we could do."

Everyone agreed, hoping for a solution to their transportation dilemma. Ethan had to get home to San Jose, California; Owen to Santa Clarita, California; Harper to Phoenix, Arizona; and Henry to Austin, Texas. All of them, industry-leading CEOs of No. 1 ranked companies, had flown in to attend this elite executive conference.

Owen interrupted a conversation about the ramifications of air travel being halted. "My friend Jimmy says he has a car we can use. They don't usually rent them, but in these unusual circumstances, he doesn't see any problem. It was repossessed a while ago, so the guy has had lots of time to make up his payments. Jimmy said we can pick it up anytime."

"Wait a minute," objected Ethan. "Are you sure it's legal?"

"We don't have any other options," confirmed Owen.

"Let's pack, get some sleep, and leave in the morning," instructed Henry, always the leader.

Jimmy had the car ready for them early the next day.

"What happens if that guy gets the money and comes back for his car?" asked Ethan, still worried about this being a smart idea.

"He's probably got another set of wheels by now," answered Jimmy. "Don't think we'll ever see his ugly face again!"

CHAPTER TWO

Harper snuggled into the back seat of their repossessed rental car heading down the I-5 freeway to their first stop in California. She flipped her thick coils of leaf-brown hair behind her shoulders. The cold drizzle was blocking the picturesque view of the mountains. She was happy to be on the way home to her secure, luxury condo overlooking the Phoenix skyline. Ethan's home in San Jose would be their first stop. He had been phoning his wife, assuring her he would be home soon. Harper thought it would be nice to have someone tall, dark, and handsome like Ethan waiting for her, but her last relationship ended a few weeks before the conference. She did not think she wanted to try another one again anytime soon. Not having slept well, she shut her eyes, trying to make her mind go blank.

The drive to Portland was uneventful, and everyone was getting hungry and needed a break. A thread of sunlight was just breaking loose between the close-knit clouds. They found a Caribbean Smoky BBQ restaurant next to a Shell gas station so Henry could also refuel the car. The hostess showed them to a secluded, comfortable, corner booth. They noticed a very quiet and somber atmosphere. It was void of the normal loud talking and laughter. As they were savoring their pulled pork sandwiches and ribs, a conversation began about where they would stop for the night.

Ethan offered a suggestion. "Sue and I stayed in a suite at the Stratford Inn in Ashland. It was very comfortable, with a delicious breakfast, and had a great fitness center and pool. It would be a relaxing break for us."

"How many more hours driving to get to Ashland?" asked Harper.

"About four and a half to five hours," answered Ethan.

"That sounds reasonable. Let's do it," Owen decided. "When we get there, I'll see if I can get a hold of my brother in New York, and I'll call Jimmy and let him know our progress."

They piled back into the car. Henry squeezed into the back with Harper, and Ethan took his turn driving. Owen settled down for a snooze beside him in the passenger seat.

"Can you move that seat up a little?" complained Henry, trying to unfold his long legs.

"Okay, Stretch," joked Owen, back to his jovial self.

It was clear sailing to Ashland. Arriving at the Stratford Inn, they were amazed at the location of this boutique hotel nestled in the foothills of the stunning mountains of Ashland. All their suites offered beautiful views with relaxing seating areas. So far, their travels were going well, and they would all be home soon. While driving through town, Harper was reminded of why they were driving a repossessed, rental car. It looked like the Fourth of July, except that the flags were flying at half-staff. She was still haunted by the memories of what she had seen when the World Trade Center towers came down. She doubted that she would be able to sleep peacefully, even in this serene setting.

They had not been settled long when Henry called a meeting in his suite. Harper and Ethan arrived, finding Henry and Owen seated at the table looking somber.

"Grab a seat," mumbled Henry. "Owen and I were checking out the car to make sure it has a good spare tire and tools. We found some interesting stuff." He reached for a duffel bag, setting it carefully in the middle of the table. Unzipping it, he reached in, bringing out a large package and setting it next to Owen.

"I'm guessing this is cocaine from the descriptions I've heard," explained Owen.

"There's much more," Henry inserted. "Weapons and ammunition. Owen found a pistol in the glovebox too."

"Well, we are going to have to turn this stuff over to the police," Ethan surmised, always wanting to do the right thing.

"Wait a minute," Henry interjected. "Think about it. With the tension regarding terrorists now and all the tightened security everywhere, they will just throw us all in jail. Who knows when we would get home, by the time we get Jimmy down here and prove it's not ours!"

"We can't be driving around with all that in the car! What if we got stopped?" expressed Ethan.

"Owen, call Jimmy and tell him what we've found and see if he has an idea of what to do," instructed Henry.

CHAPTER THREE

OWEN DIALED JIMMY'S REPOSSESSION LOT, getting his partner on the line. "Hello, Sam. Jimmy there? This is Owen checking in, and we've run into a problem," explained Owen anxiously.

There was a long pause, and it sounded like Sam was clearing his throat. A hoarse voice spoke into the phone. "Got some bad news for you, Owen!"

"Let me put you on speaker so all of us can hear you," suggested Owen. "Okay, we're ready."

Sam began painfully recalling the events of the day when he had found Jimmy in the office bludgeoned to death. "Oscar called and said he had raised the money to redeem his car and was coming in to pick it up. Jimmy called me to let me know Oscar was coming in, even though he had told him that the time period for redeeming his car had expired. Oscar claimed he didn't get a letter and was coming in anyway. I offered to come in to help, but Jimmy assured me he could handle it. I had a bad feeling, so I headed into the lot as Oscar was leaving with a bunch of papers in his hand. He jumped in his car and peeled angrily out of the lot. I ran in, calling for Jimmy, but got no answer. That's when I found him and called an ambulance, but it was too late!"

"No, no, no!" Owen cried out in anguish, running his fingers through his thick, auburn hair. "Not Jimmy!"

There was no comforting him as the shock of Jimmy's violent death settled over him. Sam warned them that Oscar probably had their paperwork and knew who they were now and where they were headed. They needed to make a plan.

"Oscar may already be on the road chasing us," Henry observed. "He may have your address in San Jose, Ethan."

"Then we better get there first," exclaimed Ethan.

"What about the cocaine and weapons, and ammunition?" interjected Harper. "We can't drive around with that in the car or let Oscar get his hands on it!"

"This guy is a very bad dude. The worst of the worst," said Henry. "We better have an ironclad plan."

Harper spoke. "I have an idea. Let's find a place to bury the weapons and all the stuff."

"Good idea," exclaimed Ethan. "We better leave now in case Oscar is on the road. We should drive straight through to San Jose. I'll let Sue know to get out of the house and stay with a friend until we get there."

Henry began taking charge and getting suitcases loaded into the car. The duffel bag was carefully hidden. Everyone grabbed snacks from the vending machines and coffee from the coffee bar. They set out again, with Owen at the wheel. They made a stop at an Ace Hardware on their way out of town to pick up a shovel. The car was eerily quiet.

Harper noted that it would be dark soon. They needed to find a remote place to take a detour and bury the duffel bag. While the others were looking at maps for places away from populated areas, Ethan was figuring out the fastest route home. He was worried that Oscar and maybe a buddy would make it there first. They could take turns driving straight through. First, he and his cohorts had serious burying to do.

CHAPTER FOUR

As they sped down the freeway, Owen was realizing the shock of his friend's death and the unbelievable situation in which they found themselves.

"Keep that speed down while we still have this illegal stuff," advised Henry from the back seat.

Owen slowed, noticing he had not been paying attention to the road.

"When we get past Mount Shasta, we might start looking for a turnoff. It's not a very populated area," offered Ethan.

Once they got past the town of Weed, they took an exit and started looking for a dirt road, hoping it would not be someone's driveway. Finally, they agreed they had gone far enough. There were no lights in sight. In the pitch dark with only a flashlight Ethan had found in the glovebox, they started taking turns digging. About six feet down seemed safe enough. Henry grabbed the duffel bag.

"Before you throw that in the hole, wouldn't it be smart to keep a couple of pistols and some ammunition for our protection?" asked Harper.

"Smart idea," complimented Henry.

After picking out their weapons, they buried the bag, covering the hole with leaves and branches. Owen covered their tracks back to the car.

Feeling some relief, they headed toward San Jose with Ethan as their guide. At the Highway 80 turnoff, they stopped for gas and some more snacks and coffee. Being familiar with the highways, Ethan decided to drive the rest of the way. His mind constantly wandered to thoughts of Sue. He had missed her so much while at the conference. He was reasonably certain she would be safe at her friend's home and have a confidante with whom she could share her thoughts on the shocking events of 9/11. He wished he had been home to hold her close and comfort her. It would not be long now.

"What is our plan when we get to Ethan's house?" questioned Harper. "What is your neighborhood like?"

Ethan described a suburban neighborhood with large trees and good-sized lots. Park areas were scattered through it. His two-story home was surrounded by hedges, with a pool and a pool house in the back yard. There were lots of places to hide.

They decided to park a few blocks away and sneak up on foot, checking to see if there was any sign of Oscar. First Ethan slowed down at the intersection and drove by the house, looking for unfamiliar cars parked on the streets. He then chose a hidden place to park. They loaded the pistols. Hopefully, they were home free and would not have to use them. Ethan took a deep breath, realizing he was putting his friends in danger.

As the four of them closed in on the expansive house, they each snuck down the outside line along the hedges, looking for any sign of light or movement. Meeting back at the car, they each reported not seeing any activity. Feeling confident that Oscar had not yet arrived, they decided to set up lookout spots from which they would wait to see if Oscar showed up. If he came onto the property, they could call the police.

Ethan drove them into the garage, taking Sue's spot for her car. They moved quietly into the kitchen, keeping the lights off while choosing the best lookout spots. Ethan led them through the downstairs, pointing out windows with good views of the perimeter of the yard. "The best views will be from upstairs," he observed, leading them up to a large balcony overlooking the living area.

Suddenly, lights flashed on. A rough voice from a corner commanded, "Drop your guns and put your hands up where I can see them…NOW!"

Startled, they dropped their guns and spun around to face the ominous voice. Their eyes focused on an acne scarred face with tobacco stained, broken teeth grinning triumphantly at them. His evil skull tattoo seemed to be mocking them, flexing from his bulging bicep.

"All of you, flat on your stomachs, hands behind your backs. Zip-tie 'em, Ty," roared Oscar, pointing his rifle at the group. "You stupid fools thought you could get away with my car!" Oscar angrily shouted. "Ty, check the car!"

Harper looked desperately over at rugged, muscular Henry, hoping he would be able to rescue them. But Henry looked helpless. Ethan lay still, his face reflecting a mind spinning with ideas of how to overpower these two thugs.

Ty bounded up the stairs. "Bag's gone, Osc!"

"Who's gunna tell me where my bag is?" demanded a scowling Oscar. "You, stand up," the man said, aggressively pointing his rifle at Harper. "What did you do with my bag?"

Harper struggled to her feet, pale, eyes wide with terror.

"Speak up, NOW!" spit Oscar.

"We…we buried it," Harper stammered.

"Where?"

"Somewhere near Mount Shasta."

"Ty, get your car. We're all going to Mount Shasta," Oscar announced.

Ethan was the closest to Oscar and was calculating how they could knock the rifle out of his hands and incapacitate him. He had to make a move before Ty got back. As quickly as he could get on his feet, he launched himself at Oscar. The deafening blast of the rifle sent Ethan flying over the balcony railing with a sickening thud below.

"Everyone downstairs!" yelled Oscar.

Ethan was lying on his side with blood beginning to soak the pure, white carpet.

"He's done," exclaimed Oscar. "Let's go!" Pointing the rifle at Henry, "You drive," he demanded.

Henry backed Oscar's car out of the garage and headed down the quiet street with Ty following. Sirens pierced the dark night in the far distance. Maybe neighbors had heard the rifle shot.

CHAPTER FIVE

NIGHT DRIVING VISIBILITY WAS GETTING worse as rain began pelting the windshield. Henry found his way back to Highway 80 and headed for the I-5 freeway, which would take them back north toward Weed. It took tremendous effort to concentrate on driving with a rifle pointed at his head. He was hoping Harper and Owen were coming up with an escape plan, and that they remembered the turnoff where they buried the drugs.

As they approached Weed, it was still pitch-black outside, making it difficult to locate the turnoff.

"Don't mess with me, guys," warned Oscar, waving the rifle around the car. "Find the road or you're dead…one at a time!"

"It's hard in the dark coming from a different direction!" exclaimed Harper. "Let's get off at Weed and head back south. Maybe it will look more familiar."

"Good idea," approved Owen. "I can hardly see the signs."

Henry took the exit to Weed, went back over the freeway, and took a left at the next intersection heading down the south I-5 entrance to the freeway. The darkness seemed oppressive, and a hopeless feeling spread over him. He knew that Oscar was not going to let them go after they found the site. He needed to protect the other two even if it meant taking life-threatening risks.

Suddenly from the back seat, "I think we just passed the road," Owen observed.

Slowing down, Henry took the next exit and started back. Crawling along the desolate, pitch-black road, they all searched for the burial spot they had chosen.

"We may have to wait until daylight to find the right place," Harper observed with a tremble in her voice.

Owen squeezed her hand, trying to give her the courage he was struggling to find.

"We'll find it tonight!" roared Oscar, seemingly frustrated with the darkness.

As they slowly progressed, Henry thought he recognized a tree close to the side of the road. "This could be it," he observed, putting on the brakes. "I remember that tree being so close to the edge of the road."

Ty slammed on the brakes behind them, and Oscar ordered everyone out of the car. "Grab the shovel, Ty," he yelled.

The wind was whipping up as they began searching with one flashlight, stumbling through the dark shrubbery.

"Don't step on a rattlesnake!" warned Henry.

"There's rattlesnakes here?" blubbered Ty. "Give me that flashlight!"

"You don't know what you're looking for, idiot," shouted Oscar. "Let Owen lead the way!"

After almost an hour of hopeless searching, Owen thought they were close enough to start digging.

"Dig!" Oscar ordered Henry. "Ty, you guard that side. You two dig with your hands," he commanded Harper and Owen.

With Oscar on one side with the rifle and Ty crazily swinging a loaded pistol, they began digging. The wind continued to increase, blowing dust into their eyes, and slowing their progress. Leaves swirled around in circles. In the distance, lightning flashed and thunder rumbled. Suddenly, a cloudburst produced a torrential downpour. They stopped digging, wiping their dripping faces. Visibility was so poor; they could barely see each other in the deluge.

Henry, seizing the opportunity, swung the shovel with all his might and strength at Ty, catching him in the face. Ty screamed, falling to the ground and clutching his nose, which was spurting a stream of blood. His weapon flew out of his hand, landing close to Harper, who lunged for it. Owen, closer to Oscar, tackled his legs, wrapping his arms around them and dragging Oscar to the ground. Startled, Oscar lost his grip on the rifle. Owen wrestled it out of his hands. He swung it wildly, hitting Oscar with a thud. Oscar rolled on the ground groaning and moaning, yelling for Ty.

The three friends sprinted toward Oscar's car, occasional lightning showing them the way. Jumping in, they sped toward the freeway.

"What do we do now?" asked Owen, gasping for breath.

"Maybe we should ditch this car," reasoned Harper.

Henry suggested they go back to Weed and see if they could trade for another car. After negotiating with a garage owner, they drove away in a newly repaired used Honda Civic. The garage owner also informed them of a motel not visible from I-5 that was located only a few miles away. Exhausted, they pulled into the motel and reserved a room facing the back parking lot. So much had happened in such a short amount of time, they just crashed on the bed and chairs. No one said a word for a few minutes, each organizing his own thoughts.

Harper broke the silence. "Do you think Ethan is dead?"

"Probably," responded Henry. "Unless those sirens got there in time."

"Let's get cleaned up and get something to eat," suggested Owen. "Then I'll drive, since my house is the next stop."

They took turns showering and then headed for the motel's restaurant. The waitress serving them asked if they had heard the latest news from New York. Survivors were being pulled out of the rubble. Some firefighters and civilians who had survived had made cell phone calls from the voids beneath the rubble and debris. After listening to her report of the latest news and having a good, hot meal, they started to revive a little.

"We need some sleep," yawned Harper.

"We could take turns driving and napping," said Henry.

CHAPTER SIX

THE WEATHER STARTED TO IMPROVE as they started out on their eight-and-a-half-hour drive to Santa Clarita. It was developing into a sunny afternoon. With the freeway dry and visibility high, they made good time. Harper curled up in the back seat, and Henry put the passenger seat back as far as it would go. Reclining the back of the seat and stretching his legs out, he was soon softly snoring. With Owen at the wheel, the car peacefully hummed down the freeway. Thoughts of Jimmy and Ethan filled Owen's thoughts with regret and sadness. Sadness turned to anger as he wondered how badly Ty and Oscar had been hurt. Seriously, he hoped.

Once Henry and Harper roused from napping, Owen brought up the subject they had been avoiding. "You really clobbered that Ty a good one!" he commented, glancing at Henry.

"He'll be looking at one ugly face for the rest of his miserable life," laughed Henry.

"If he's still alive," interjected Harper. "You saved our lives, Henry!"

"It took all of us as a team," responded Henry, sincerely. "Those guys should be out of commission for a while!"

"Thank, God," exclaimed Harper. "I've had enough death threats to last me a lifetime!"

"Who knew attending this conference would turn out so eventful?" joked Owen.

"I'm due for a stop soon," Harper informed Owen.

Stopping for gas and lunch at Denny's gave them time to relax and unwind. Tension had gripped them since the first Trade Center tower impalement and collapse.

"I'm going to try to get my brother again in New York," Owen suggested after lunch.

Henry and Harper took the opportunity to take a short walk down a berm along a scenic river flowing behind Denny's through the quaint town. Surprising Harper, Henry reached for her, firmly gripping her hand.

"Harper, you are the smartest and most courageous woman I know!"

Speechless, Harper smiled and squeezed his hand. A warm, tingling feeling spread through her. "Thank you, Henry, for such a beautiful compliment. Owen is probably done with his call by now. We'd better get back," she said, gently slipping her hand away. They slowly walked back, both realizing a deeper connection had just been formed between them.

"I talked to my brother!" Owen exclaimed, happy and relieved. He described to them his brother's account of the chaos and disruptions in the city. Getting to work was proving to be impossible with the central district barricaded, not to mention the emotional fears and anxiety people were experiencing. They were helping where they could with support from friends, neighbors, and spiritual communities.

"He's doing well," stated Owen as they walked toward the car.

CHAPTER SEVEN

"**I**'ll drive the next stretch," volunteered Henry, "While you take a nap, Owen."

Harper sat up front with Henry so Owen could stretch out in the back. Having talked to his brother and now almost home, Owen easily fell asleep.

While Owen slept, Henry and Harper talked quietly, telling each other about their lives and families. Henry described the CEO responsibilities required of him for his company. Harper recounted her difficult climb to the top as a woman. Listening to her story reaffirmed Henry's appreciation for her bravery, intelligence, and resilience. He also loved the way caramel ribbon highlights complemented her brunette hair as it tumbled over her shoulders, as well as the chic way she dressed.

As Henry drove, Harper stole glances at him, admiring his strong rugged looks and his blond hair shining in the sunlight. She recognized his leadership qualities, analytical abilities, and thoughtfulness. Maybe dark and handsome wasn't what she wanted after all. There was a comfortable trust between them. The scenery flew past them unnoticed.

When Owen woke up, they took another needed break before heading down the last stretch to his home in Santa Clarita, just north of Los Angeles.

"I'll drive the rest of the way," stated Owen, knowing the route well. The sun had set. Darkness settled in as they traveled, and they listened to the country music that Owen had turned on. Each had thoughts of things that had to be done when they got home—mounds of catch-up work and fires to put out.

The car was droning on when Owen broke the peaceful mood. "That guy has been on my tail for a few miles now."

"Speed up and see what he does," recommended Henry.

Owen sped up, keeping an eye on the rearview mirror. The car behind quickly caught up again. Alarmed, he moved into the fast lane. The other car slowed, and Owen eventually moved back into the slow lane, thinking he was too jumpy after all the events of the past days. Without warning, a car roared up the fast lane, then slowed directly next to Owen. A wobbling rifle poked out the passenger window.

"Ty!" Harper screamed.

Owen slammed on the brakes. Ty's car shot out down the fast lane, swerving right in front of Owen. Owen cranked the wheel, sideswiping Ty's car, sending both cars flipping over and over down the steep ravine at the side of the freeway. One car exploded into flames.

All was quiet except for the roar of the fire. Harper thought she heard a groan and realized it was her. The battered car was resting on its roof. She was awkwardly hanging in her seatbelt, the airbag supporting her side. Trying to twist to release the seatbelt caused her sudden shooting pain.

"Henry, Owen," she called, but got no response.

She felt warm and dizzy, and the smell was awful. Slowly blackness enveloped her, and her body relaxed, hanging limply from her seatbelt.

CHAPTER EIGHT

Harper opened her blurry eyes to see two firefighters' concerned faces as they carried her to a waiting ambulance.

"Henry, Owen," she weakly whispered.

"They're okay," comforted one firefighter.

Harper closed her eyes, succumbing to the relief from the pain medication given to her in the ambulance. Arrival at the emergency room at the Santa Clarita Hospital was hazy, but she knew she was alive. Harper woke up the following morning having spent part of the long night in surgery repairing broken bones in her left arm and shoulder. It took her a few moments to take in her surroundings. She recalled the horrific accident. Sudden panic set in. Sweat began to form on her forehead, and she began to tremble. A couple of nurses rushed in, checking her heart rate and blood pressure.

"Where are Henry and Owen?" she spluttered shakily.

"One is in the room next to you, and one is in intensive care," replied the black nurse gently.

Later that day, Harper was resting with her eyes closed, happy that both Henry and Owen were alive. She thought she heard a familiar voice call out, "Harper."

Opening her eyes, she said, "Henry?"

"I'm down here," he said, reaching up from his wheelchair to grab her hand.

"What happened to you?" she asked.

"Just a broken leg and lots of bruises!"

"I'm so glad you're okay," she cried, tears running down her face. He gently kissed her hand, his lips lingering tenderly.

Experiencing some brain trauma, Owen was in intensive care for a few days. As soon as he was released to a room, Henry and Harper planned a visit. With Harper walking, her arm in a cast and shoulder supported with a sling, and Henry rolling his wheelchair, they quietly entered Owen's room.

"Henry, Harper!" Owen cried out. "Am I ever glad to see you two!"

"We're a little banged up, but alive!" expressed Henry.

"What happened to the other two?" questioned Owen.

"They didn't make it," answered Harper slowly, remembering the heat from the fire.

"Well, we can go on with our lives now. Except for Ethan," Owen responded sadly.

The door to Owen's room opened a crack, and a nurse stuck her head in. "Can you handle more visitors?"

In walked Ethan, holding the hand of a beautiful young lady. "Let me introduce you to Sue, my wife. The ambulance got there in time," he said to their gaping faces.

Everyone smiled, laughed, cried, and hugged as best they could.

"What a wonderful reunion!" exclaimed Harper.

"We have a bond that will never be broken!" expressed Henry solemnly.

Owen looked fondly around at his beat-up conference group. "The doctor is letting me rehabilitate at home. I have a large ranch in the valley with room for all of you to stay for a few days. I think we all need a little spoiling by my housekeeper and chef."

Everyone agreed, and it was decided.

CHAPTER NINE

The next day, Ethan and Sue brought Owen home, and everyone met at his ranch house. It was a whole wonderful week of telling funny stories, laughing, and relaxing on the sumptuous patio furniture, and eating their favorite dishes. The ranch was nestled in a beautiful valley surrounded by rolling hills. It was quiet. Horses came up to the fence begging for apples. They began to feel their stress rolling away. Once a day, Owen had physical therapy. A counselor came twice to sit and talk with them about their traumatic experiences. They all decided to meet again the same week the next year for a reunion. By then, they believed they would all be healed and back to normal lives.

It was a sad farewell. Ethan and Sue were going back to San Jose to put their house up for sale. They were looking at condos closer to his work. Owen would go back to work after a few more weeks of rehabilitation. Harper and Henry still had to get home. Owen gave them one of his cars for the trip. Everyone hugged and wished each other well. They understood, as they were dealing with their own trauma, the country was reeling from the impacts of September 11. There were going to be difficult days ahead as the dangerous work to recover the dead continued. Speeches would be made. Heart breaking memorials would be held. There would be unprecedented demands on New York's public health care. The environmental assault would disperse hazardous particles in the air for months to come. Terrorism is an assault on the mental health and well-being of the public. It creates panic, fear, and anxiety. Those hugs and well wishes were going to be greatly appreciated during the future dark hours of uncertainty.

CHAPTER TEN

"Good thing it's only my left leg that is broken," Henry observed as he climbed in the driver's seat.

"It's great to be heading home," expressed Harper as she sat next to him. "Don't push yourself. If you get tired, we can stay overnight halfway. I can't drive with my broken arm."

Henry grinned. "It's only six hours. I can drive that with a broken leg, easy!"

Despite their injuries, they were feeling somewhat positive, both looking forward to getting home and back to work.

Soon they were headed east on I-10, cruising through the hot desert, air conditioning blasting.

"Do you have room for me to stay overnight at your condo, or should I reserve a hotel room?" Henry asked Harper.

"Do you mind sleeping on the couch?" she responded.

"Not at all, especially if it means spending more time together," observed Henry.

Harper smiled, remembering the brief tingling feeling when he took her hand while walking on the berm. Feeling warm and hopeful, she closed her eyes and rested her head back, imagining what could lie ahead for them. Rousing when Henry pulled into a gas station, Harper called her housekeeper. She would make sure the condo was ready for their arrival and stock the fridge.

Excited to be so close to home, Harper and Henry talked nonstop until the impressive Phoenix skyline came in to view. Pulling up under the canopy of Harper's condominium building, Henry turned off the car, giving the keys to the valet.

"Hi, Dan," Harper greeted the doorman. "How are you?"

"I'm fine. What happened to your arm?" he questioned, looking very concerned.

"We were in an accident, but I'm on the mend now!" she informed him. "I would like you to meet Henry. Henry, meet Dan."

The two men shook hands.

Dan began to unload their luggage. "I'll bring it right up for you."

Harper expressed her thanks as they walked into the stunning foyer. Surrounded by glass, palm trees created a tropical border. Bright-colored pots exploded with Chinese Hibiscus, Red Ginger, Orchids, and Anthuriums. The gorgeous room, dripping with Passionflower and Jasmine vines, gave a feeling of stepping into the jungle. Scattered benches sat under the palms, beckoning passersby to sit and rest by the Angel Wing Begonias.

"Wow, this is amazing!" exclaimed Henry, taking in the sweet smell of the Jasmine.

"I love lingering here after work. It makes me relax and leave the office behind," Harper mused.

Entering the elevator, she pushed the eighth-floor button.

CHAPTER ELEVEN

HARPER TURNED THE KEY AND opened her condo door. It was the gateway into where she felt safe and could be herself. Her efficient housekeeper had already turned on the air conditioning. It felt cool and inviting. A beautiful vase of Fire and Ice Roses was centered on the modern dining table. On the coffee table waited a chilled bottle of champagne, glasses, and a basket filled with fresh fruit and her favorite white chocolate chip cookies. Harper looked around. "Before we dive into all that, we need a good meal! I'll order Chinese. Make yourself at home."

She headed for her bedroom, taking an awkward, warm shower while holding her arm out of the spray. After changing into a comfortable, silky red lounging caftan, she ordered dinner.

They feasted on Harper's delicious takeout food, then Henry showered and changed from his travel clothes. Finding Harper relaxed on the couch with her feet tucked under her, he sat carefully beside her, keeping his casted leg away.

"You look so beautiful sitting there," he commented. "Ready to celebrate with some champagne?"

He had shaved, and he smelled of her Caribbean shower gel. His blond hair, still damp, curled lazily above his sparkling blue eyes.

"You're quite handsome yourself," she blushed.

Henry poured the chilled champagne, and they munched on cookies, happy to be together, talking and laughing, and enjoying each other's company.

"Well, you have a long drive tomorrow. We better get to bed," Harper finally interrupted their beautiful evening.

Bringing out blankets and pillows for Henry, she laid them on the couch. Reaching up, Henry pulled her down to him. His lips gently found hers. They were lilac soft. She eagerly submitted to his kiss, shivers tingling up her spine. He pulled her close, holding her carefully without pressure on her arm or shoulder.

"I believe I've fallen in love with you," he whispered in her ear.

In response, Harper kissed him deeply and longingly. Wrapped securely in Henry's arms, they slept together, moving into Harper's luxurious bed until the morning light filtered through the blinds.

Henry woke to the smell of bacon and coffee. Harper was cooking a delicious breakfast before his long drive home.

"Morning," he greeted, kissing her adoringly. "When we get these casts off, we'll make a night of it."

"Once you are settled in back at work, you're welcome to visit any time," she invited.

"I'll be back as soon as possible," he promised, sipping his steaming coffee.

Between bites, they talked of the future. Henry wanted to introduce Harper to his family at Thanksgiving. She responded with an invitation to spend the week after Christmas with her family at a Puerto Penasco beach resort in Mexico. With lots of exciting ideas and plans for the months ahead, they reluctantly called Dan to collect Henry's luggage and the valet to bring the car out front.

Henry held Harper close as they lovingly kissed, not wanting to separate. He took her hand as they walked to the elevator, kissing again as the doors closed. In the foyer jungle, they held each other, one last kiss, and reluctantly said their good-byes.

CHAPTER TWELVE –

One Year Later

Their lives had crossed at meaningful and dangerous intersections, suddenly connecting them, and changing their futures forever.

It was their year reunion. The conference group of four, who watched the horror of 9/11 while in Seattle, was together again. The four, who faced the wrath of Oscar and Ty, were chased, shot at, and left for dead. Now they would celebrate the unbreakable bond that had formed between them. They were meeting again a year after they had spent a valuable week together, recuperating at Owen's sprawling ranch in Santa Clarita.

Owen waited in front of his massive double doors, looking past the flowing entry steps. His brother from New York stood next to him. They watched the stretch limo drive slowly through the gate. The lush green lawns outlined the long driveway curving up to the house, which was graced with garden beds bursting with pure white roses. Owen and his brother Matt walked out to greet everyone. Ethan and Sue hugged them, followed by Henry and Harper who walked hand in hand. Owen's big bear hugs made everyone feel warm and welcome. They made their way through the rich, sprawling house to the back patio. Feeling like they had come home, they sank into the sumptuous seating, sipping their drinks and enjoying a delicious lite lunch.

Each told of the past year—the struggles, changes, and accomplishments. Owen had taken longer to recuperate than planned, so he took a job with less stress with the same company. Matt moved in with him and was also hired by his company.

Ethan and Sue had sold their home where he was shot by Oscar and left for dead. They purchased a condo with a fantastic security system close to his work. Six months ago they had a baby girl, Ava, who was staying with her grandparents while Ethan and Sue attended the reunion.

Henry and Harper talked about their trip home and falling in love. After a few months, they had decided to have Harper move into Henry's luxury home in the Reserve at Lake Travis. She had found a perfect job with a great corporation and was already thriving there.

Eventually, each member of the group shared their struggles with the aftermath of their traumatic experiences. Owen had struggled with guilt and grief at the loss of his friend who loaned them the car in Seattle. For a while, they had all experienced fearful moments and difficulty sleeping. Owen was recovering from depression he developed during his long recuperation. However, they were all survivors. They were highly resilient, and had developed appropriate coping strategies. With family and social supports, they all agreed they were functioning effectively in the various areas of their lives.

They spent their time together celebrating each other and decided to meet again the next year.

Best of all, they would soon be meeting in Austin for a Thanksgiving wedding.

PART TWO:

DANGEROUS CONNECTIONS

Before you embark on a journey of revenge – dig two graves.

CONFUCIUS

CHAPTER THIRTEEN

On a hot, sultry, early morning on the amazing Bay of Banderas, the shopkeepers glanced up to see Senores Conroy jogging along the El Malecon. His pace was fiercely intense. It was high tide and windy. As he ran along the famous coastal boardwalk, waves thundered against the rocks, splashing him with the cool surf. He could taste the salty spray. His morning routine never changed.

The seafront promenade was all but deserted at this time of the day. Soon it would be swarming with curious tourists enjoying the old downtown Puerto Vallarta, El Centro area. The beachside walkway was populated with numerous interesting, and amazing statues and sculptures. Shopkeepers were preparing their displays to tempt tourists to spend freely. Hanging as backdrops were Mayan wooden masks and gorgeous textiles. Shelves were loaded with brightly painted pottery, dishes, tiles, and wall art. Display cases showed off delicate Taxco silver jewelry. For the delight of the palate, few would be able to resist the Mexican vanilla, made from the orchid flower. Customers would also enjoy hot salsa, liqueurs, tequilas, and Kahlua. Senores Conroy, as the locals called him, noticed none of these exciting elements, as he concentrated exclusively on his form and his breathing.

A sweat soaked cap was pulled down to protect the sensitive skin on Conroy's face from the burning sun. By the time the shops, markets, bars, restaurants, and cafes opened, he would be back and over the wide, generous pedestrian bridge spanning the river Cuale, heading south toward his condo

Conroy reached the street entrance of his beach-front condo building, jogging past the darkened bar area, taking the stairs two at a time up to the fourth floor. Putting in his door code, he entered his hiding place where he felt safe and secure. Heading straight for his well-stocked kitchen, he filled a tall glass with low-fat chocolate milk, refueling his exhausted muscles.

In less than an hour, Conroy was down the stairways and out on the soft, white, sandy beach. Senores Sergio, Conroy's neighbor, was out on his luxurious covered balcony, sipping his strong, steaming, morning Mexican coffee. He expected Conroy to appear at any moment for his rigorous daily ocean swim.

Conroy dove into the choppy waves, swimming back and forth, parallel to the beach. Sergio wondered why Conroy never wore a swimsuit. He swam with long shorts and a long-sleeved shirt, probably for UV protection. His strokes were not a slicing, smooth freestyle, but rather giant, muscle-building butterfly strokes. Sergio could see back muscles bulging through Conroy's wet shirt, as he propelled his body forward, fighting the relentless waves. Soon, Conroy headed for the shore, wrapping himself in a towel and resting in a lounge chair that was shaded under a thatched-roof palapa. Sergio studied him and wondered who this solitary, unusual man was, and why he was so obsessively driven.

Conroy spent the rest of his day in the cool comfort of his condo, preparing homework to be turned in at his evening class. He was studying corporate accounting. He had already passed the CPA (Certified Public Accountant) exam. Now he was working on specializing his skills, learning how to analyze data to support business decision-making, financial reporting, budgeting, and forecasting. When his training was complete, his plan was to apply to a corporation in the Los Angeles area.

After Conroy's evening class, he stopped by the bar in his building for his favorite drink, Xtabentun liqueur. This delicate, sweet spirit was the only treat he allowed himself. Rosa saw him under the streetlight and had his usual drink ready for him at the bar. She had tried flirting with this swarthy, handsome man. He bought her a drink once, but that was as far as it had gone.

Back safe in his condo, with only the sound of the crashing waves, Conroy congratulated himself on another day well spent. He was getting close to his goal. For a year and a-half he had not taken his eye off the prize. Fury would burn in his soul until the much-anticipated day of his revenge.

CHAPTER FOURTEEN

Owen and Matt had settled comfortably into their life on Owen's ranch in Santa Clarita, just north of Los Angeles. The brothers had gone through unbelievable trauma to get to this point.

A year and a-half ago, Matt was living in New York city on that fateful day, 9/11, when the Twin Towers were attacked. Once air travel had been restored, he had come to California to spend some time with his brother, Owen. Matt's short visit became longer. Eventually, he moved in to stay.

Owen had experienced his own trauma after 9/11 on his way home from a CEO conference held in Seattle. Inviting Matt to stay worked out well for both of them. They supported each other through their struggles with the aftermath of their horrific ordeals. Owen, finding his CEO position too demanding, took a less stressful job with his corporation in the business development department. Matt also secured a position in Owen's corporation. He was a perfect fit for the human resource department. They both enjoyed their jobs and never complained about going to work.

Despite loving their jobs, Owen and Matt looked forward to heading home each day to their sprawling valley ranch, surrounded by three mountain ranges. Their acreage bordered pastures and horse ranches. Driving through the gates and up the long, curved driveway, outlined with lush, green lawns, gave them the feeling of peace and calm. It seemed like they were shutting out the mad world and leaving it behind.

Owen and Matt had a daily routine. After arriving home, they enjoyed a relaxing dip in their sixty-foot pool. It was steps away from their expansive patio which ran the full length of the house. On one end was a sumptuous seating area with sheer, sky-blue curtains between the posts, blowing in the gentle breeze. In the middle was a gorgeous western red cedar table with seating for twenty. The other end was an outdoor kitchen and bar area. Now, their chef Eric was preparing a healthy and delicious evening meal while they were unwinding.

In the massive side yard, Owen had a pickle-ball court installed. Later, in the cool evening, he and Matt usually played a few highly competitive games.

In the mornings, Matt jogged along the roads winding between the ranches. Owen preferred to work out in their well-appointed gym. Then their workday would begin again.

While they were at work, their chef, Eric, and house manager, Maria, took care of the daily home responsibilities. Eric shopped and planned meals which were often prepared for entertaining guests. Maria had been taking business and office skills training classes at night school. She had taken over the organization of scheduling workers, landscape crews, and pool caretakers, as well as the housecleaning staff. Now, with her computer skills, she could prepare spreadsheets, keeping track of expenses and reports for Owen. When there were large groups to entertain, Maria would help Eric with the serving and clean-up.

Besides the three-car garage attached to the house, there was a detached three-car garage in the side yard opposite the pickle-ball court. Eric had room for his Land Rover. The second garage space was for a car Owen gave to Maria to use, and the third space was for the riding mower, golf cart, and storage. Attached to the garages was the pool cabana. That made lots of room on a second floor where Eric and Maria had their own cozy apartments. They were both hard workers and took two days off during the week, since the weekends usually ended up being busy with people coming and going.

Often, Owen and Matt would invite coworkers to their home for a rousing game of pickle-ball or a game of volleyball in the pool. The area beyond the patio was designed as a tropical oasis with a freeform pool. The light-colored interior surface of the pool gave the feeling of the crystalline waters of an island. Lush green palms and ferns and vibrant colored flowers added to the delightful tropical haven. The pool deck was complete with outdoor loungers and hammocks for relaxing. A rock walkway led through the bougainvillea hedges to the cabana, which contained a changing room with a couple of showers. The entrance could be closed off with a wall of folding panels, or left completely open. They often used it as a home cinema, showing their favorite movies.

Owen and Matt loved to entertain and had a houseful of guests at least once a week. Owen naturally attracted friends with his warm, jovial nature. Unlike Owen, Matt was tall, lean, and muscular. His quick wit and generosity caused him to be well liked at work. Their home was known for its welcoming, fun atmosphere.

It was soon time for a second reunion of Owen's Seattle CEO conference group. The four of them, their flights grounded, had driven back to their homes after 9/11 in a rented, repossessed car. The terror they survived on that road trip had changed their futures forever. Their connection was a special one. They kept in touch, offering each other support and friendship. They promised to meet every year at Owen's ranch. All of them were looking forward to seeing each other, hugging, and spending priceless time hanging out together. Unknown to them, the shocking revelations at this upcoming second reunion would shatter their lives again.

CHAPTER FIFTEEN

THE BREEZE WAS GENTLE TODAY as Conroy raced down the El Malecon ocean-side boardwalk. The bay was calm. Early morning was the quiet part of the day before the markets and shops opened. Conroy quickened his pace in anticipation of the taxing, challenging day ahead. After his invigorating ocean swim, he would be venturing out on his weekly trip into the vast, mysterious Sierra Madre Mountain jungle.

The imposing mountain range created a majestic, epic backdrop for the city of Puerto Vallarta. Abundant rainforests reached down, touching many of the beaches around the bay. Valleys and canyons provided tourists opportunities to experience thrilling zip-lines and suspended rope bridges, soaring high up through the canopy. Other trips included rappelling down breathtaking waterfalls, enchanting birdwatching of over 350 bird species, hair-raising ATV trips, and riveting animal viewing hikes where the tourists could search for monkeys, parrots, iguanas, armadillos, and ocelots. Or, they just relaxed on a white-sand beach, sipping margaritas, waves lapping at their feet.

Completing his morning exercise routine, Conroy walked a few blocks from his condo. His Jeep Wrangler was kept in a secluded garage off the main street in a nearby alley. His adventure began with a stop to stock up on food supplies and bottled water. Then it was a bumpy ride over the cobblestone streets leading directly up into the vast mountains. After a fifteen-minute drive into the jungle, Conroy spotted a parking lot with a couple of tour buses. A trail led from there to the location where the Predator movie jungle scene was filmed. It included a crashed helicopter onto which people could climb.

After about an hour driving up the winding mountain road, Conroy took an unmarked turnoff. The pavement soon faded to dirt and ruts, then mud and rocks, causing teeth-jarring bumps. Not far down the road was a river he needed to ford. The rainy season was not in full swing yet, so maybe he could find a shallow crossing. The bridge had been washed out in a deluge during last year's hurricane.

Stopping at the river's edge, Conroy stepped down from his jeep. He paced up and down the bank, assessing the depth of the water using familiar trees and bushes for reference. He decided on what he thought to be the shallowest crossing. He put the jeep in low gear with the lowest revs possible. Slowly and gently, he drove into the water, keeping his momentum smooth and steady. This kept him from getting a huge, bow wave up over the bonnet, risking a flooded engine. Eventually, he crawled up the opposite bank and back onto the wild road. After a bone-crunching half hour of driving, he came to a large clearing with an electric fence stretching around it. He stopped, looking up the mountain to see a man with a grey, bushy beard, jogging down toward the rustic gate.

"Hola, Carlos," Conroy called to him.

"Bienvenido, Senores Conroy," Carlos welcomed, his scarred face broadening into a wide grin.

Carlos was wearing his favorite sleeveless shirt, sporting a band of skulls tattooed around his biceps. He jumped into the passenger seat of the jeep after closing the gate behind them. They parked in front of a ramshackle house, which seemed to have suffered from years of neglect. They unloaded the supplies Conroy had brought, taking them into a surprising state-of-the-art kitchen. Bright pottery dishes lined the open shelves. Graceful arches led to comfortable rooms with bold colors and rustic furnishings, with cultural influences. It gave the home a multifarious feel, mixing rustic wood and wrought iron furniture, blending authentic art and textiles.

Carlos was very well off, having worked for the drug cartels since his retirement from the Mexican Army. For months, he had been teaching Conroy how to make all types of bombs. In the army, Carlos had been known as their explosive's expert. Conroy had accompanied him on various bombing assignments, honing his skills. They had met at a bar in the city and became immediate, fast friends.

Today, Carlos and Conroy were headed farther up the mountain to practice sniper training. They secured their bulletproof vests and snapped on walkie-talkies. They dressed in their jungle camouflage outfits, so as to draw as little attention as possible. There were often military lookouts in the surrounding hills, giving updates on any activity in the area.

"Let's get going, Amigo," ordered Carlos.

They sprayed themselves generously with mosquito repellant, then set off, heading up the mountain. They passed a shed where Carlos' black Ford Raptor was parked. Then they walked through another secured gate and onto a pathway into the jungle. Reaching the rifle range, Conroy positioned his .50-caliber sniper rifle and followed Carlos' expert instructions. They practiced firing, aiming at various targets spaced at longer-than-usual ranges. Carlos was confident in Conroy's marksmanship, and impressed with his skilled ability to adjust to any environmental conditions.

Arriving back at Carlos' home, they feasted on the delicious Ceviche that Conroy had brought. The seafood was fresh from the bay and cured to perfection. Crispy tostadas and spicy salsas complemented the meal.

Conroy did not want to say good-bye to his best friend and faithful trainer. Unfortunately, the time had come to make the long-awaited move to Los Angeles. Carlos had many connections who had provided all the papers Conroy needed—passports, university degrees, work history, and references. Finally, all was in place. He was ready for his burning mission.

Carlos wished him good luck. "Buena suerte!"

They parted with a hardy hug and a good-bye kiss on the cheek.

"Gracias, Carlos," expressed Conroy, gratefully.

"Hasta la vista!" exclaimed Carlos.

CHAPTER SIXTEEN

Owen and Matt turned out of the driveway, heading to their Valencia corporate building. The sky was clear radiant blue, as if an artist had brushed away the clouds. It was Friday. A group of co-workers were coming over after work to celebrate Anna's birthday. The twelve of them got along well and enjoyed fierce pickleball competitions. They had formed an easy camaraderie and usually met every couple of weeks at Owen and Matt's house. This week would be a special celebration, so Eric, their chef, was preparing a festive dinner.

"I'm looking forward to the party tonight," commented Owen.

"It'll be great!" responded Matt. "By the way, I was thinking about this new guy I hired for the accounting department. He's pretty sharp and seems like a really nice guy. I was wondering what you would think of inviting him to join us. It might be a chance for him to get to know some people."

"Sure, see if he can come. I'll let Eric know. What's his name?"

"Conroy."

The workday went by quickly. Conroy happily accepted Matt's invitation. Throughout the day, every time Conroy thought about the invite, he could not believe his good luck. His plan was falling into place faster than he had expected. He would make this evening count. The anticipation was making him nervous, so he just focused on his new job. He had gotten along well with Matt and now he was going to be a guest in Matt and Owen's home. He would have to be careful not to make any mistakes.

Finding his way to the sprawling ranch was easy for Conroy. He already knew the way. For days he had mapped out the neighborhood. He knew all the roads going in and out. When he arrived at the gate, he pressed the intercom button and stated his name. Driving in, he parked alongside the other guests. Matt showed him through the expansive house to the back patio where Maria was taking orders for drinks.

"Hey, everyone. I'd like you to meet Conroy. Introduce yourself to him. He's new in accounting," explained Matt.

"Hi, Conroy. I'm Maria. Follow me to the bar and we'll get you set up with a drink," invited Maria.

"Thank you. It's nice to meet you," Conroy graciously accepted.

Conroy joined the group in the seating area of the patio. They were relaxing, talking, and laughing after a demanding work week. He looked around, envious of their obvious close friendships. Owen was recording how each one preferred his prime rib to pass on to Eric. Maria was serving delicious looking appetizers. Conroy noticed her outgoing, friendly, and cheerful personality. Her delicate facial features were complemented by her dark, magnetic eyes. Long black hair fell loosely over her tanned shoulders. Conroy admired her graceful movements as she interacted comfortably with each guest. Maybe he would get a chance to talk to her later.

Soon Matt seated everyone at the table in the center of the patio. They feasted on prime rib roast, loaded baked potatoes, and a perfect avocado salad. It was a stunning evening with the sun dropping behind the mountains. Lights twinkled around the patio. Automatic lights were coming on, shining throughout the lush, tropical gardens. The pool lights made the water shimmer and glow in the twilight. No one suspected any evil intentions lurking in such a peaceful setting.

Large double doors opened from the patio to the recreation room where everyone hung out playing pool and ping pong, or talking at the bar. Owen entertained them while Matt helped Eric and Maria clean up.

Matt interrupted the fun. "Okay, everyone, follow me to the cabana!"

They followed him past the pool and down the pathway lined with bougainvillea. Maria turned on the lights, revealing streamers, balloons, and a sparkling sign that read, "Happy Birthday, Anna." They all cheered and sang "Happy Birthday." Anna's blue eyes shone, dancing with surprise and delight. She looked over at Owen, and said, "Thank you!"

Anna was smart and attractive with flowing blond hair and a smile that lit up her face. Even though she was a little reserved, Owen had been getting to know her at their group get-togethers. They got along well and found they had a lot in common. They also made a hard pickleball team to beat!

"We have a gift for you," Owen said as he handed her an exquisitely, wrapped box.

In the box, Anna found a ticket to a baseball game at Dodger Stadium.

"We all went together and got you a Field Box seat, but we're not going to let you go alone! We're all going with you," announced Owen.

"What a perfect gift! Thank you all," Anna gushed, giving Owen a warm hug.

To top off the party, Maria and Matt served coffee. Eric brought in his masterpiece, Red Velvet Cake, which just happened to be Anna's favorite.

When the celebrating was over, some decided to go for a swim, while the other guests hung out in the cabana. Owen and Anna sat talking, laughing, and enjoying each other's company. Matt went to check on the clean-up progress in the kitchen. As he rounded a corner, he almost bumped into Conroy. Startled, he offered, "Conroy, anything I can get for you?"

"No, thank you. I was looking for the bathroom," Conroy replied.

"There's one down the hall and one in the cabana too!"

"Thank you. You have a beautiful home. I appreciate you inviting me."

"Would you like a tour? I'm sure Maria would be happy to show you around," extended Matt.

Maria showed Conroy around the house, answering his many questions. He thanked her and his hosts and said his good nights. Things were winding down and soon all the guests had left.

Owen, Matt, Eric, and Maria relaxed with a night cap on the patio seating. They liked to talk over the evening's events after people left, recalling how everything went. They agreed it was a successful party for Anna.

"Conroy asked a lot of personal questions when I took him on a tour. It made me feel a little uneasy," expressed Maria.

"I was wondering if he was wandering around the house when I almost bumped into him," said Matt.

"He was probably just curious about the place. Maybe he is not used to such a big house," observed Owen.

"Well, I hope he got to know some of the group. That should help him feel more comfortable at work," said Matt.

Stretching and yawning, Owen thanked them for all their hard work, Eric for a fabulous dinner, Maria for decorating the cabana, and Matt for making it all run smoothly. Owen and Eric turned in for the night. Matt and Maria talked into the early morning hours.

CHAPTER SEVENTEEN

Conroy was enjoying his accounting job and worked diligently to make a good impression. Usually, after work he went home to his loft apartment in a nondescript building on the edge of the industrial district. Being an unmemorable, common looking building was perfect for him, as he did not want to draw any attention. The inside of his loft was a completely different story. The 1500 square-foot space was finished up in an industrial style, with steel beams and exposed brick and pipes. It was one large, open space without internal walls—aside from the bathroom. The space was unique with its rustic touches. One side featured wall-to-ceiling windows with incredible views of the Los Angeles skyline. It was sparsely furnished since Conroy did not expect to be staying there for long.

Another benefit of the location of Conroy's loft was that it was close to his loyal friend, Francisco, whose warehouse was only a few blocks away. Francisco ran a drug trafficking business through legitimate business enterprises he had developed over the years. Enormous amounts of cocaine, meth, heroin, and fentanyl were smuggled from Mexico through his sophisticated network. The drugs were hidden in the trucks he used to import legitimate products. Francisco made millions through working with various Mexican drug cartels. He used all that money to fund a lucrative life of yachts, horses, and luxury cars. In a few days, Conroy was expecting a package of supplies from Carlos, arriving from Puerto Vallarta in one of Francisco's trucks.

Conroy had been invited back to Owen and Matt's ranch for various get-togethers. He was learning to play pickleball. Being athletic and strong, he was a quick study and mastered the skills he needed to be competitive. Conroy also enjoyed visiting with Maria. She had grown up in a small beach town north of Puerto Vallarta on the Bay of Banderas. When Maria found out Conroy had lived there for a short while, she loved visiting with him. She missed her home. They talked about all the wonderful, amazing features of the area—the stunning bay, the jaw-dropping sunsets, the jungle and waterfalls, and the friendly people. Most of all, they both missed the mouth-watering food sold by the local street vendors.

Other days Conroy just watched. He would park behind a hill across from a horse pasture, near Owen's ranch property. From the top of the hill, he had an unobstructed view of the ranch and the surrounding countryside. He would lie beside a huge boulder with shrubs hiding him, as he watched with his powerful binoculars. He watched people come and go, learned schedules for workers, and memorized the roads coming in and out. He was patient. He carefully and meticulously developed his plans.

The day finally came when Francisco called to let Conroy know that his package had arrived. He rushed over to the warehouse after work. They warmly greeted each other with a kiss on the cheek. Francisco stood tall, looking handsome in his custom-made navy-blue suit. His thick, dark hair had a stylish cut.

"Como estas?" Francisco asked.

"I'm doing very well now," Conroy responded enthusiastically. "Look at my new teeth," he said grinning to show them off. "Your sister did a wonderful job fixing them for me!"

"They look great," admired Francisco. "She's a good dentist."

"I appreciated you sending me to her," thanked Conroy.

They walked between massive racks of new furniture to the back of the warehouse where Francisco had a tiny office. He handed Conroy a bulky, heavy package.

"Carlos said to wish you well and lots of luck," Francisco passed on. "When you get tired of that boring accounting job, come back to work for us," he invited.

"I'll let you know. Thank you," said Conroy.

They walked to the back loading docks where Conroy had parked. Placing the package in the trunk, he carefully drove home, his heart crazily beating with excitement and anticipation. He opened the garage door with his remote, waiting until it shut securely behind him before getting out of the car. His private elevator was steps away. It opened directly into his loft. He pressed a clock on the wall which activated a sliding door into his workshop. Placing the package in a secure, fire-resistant floor safe, he left the room and closed the door. He would begin his delicate work tomorrow.

Carlos' training was now going to pay off. Conroy felt that all the months of brutal preparation would be worth it in the end. There would finally be a long-awaited accounting for the agonizing suffering he had endured.

CHAPTER EIGHTEEN

It was unusually early for Matt to be heading to work. He did his early morning run through the countryside roads and grabbed a lite breakfast. He was driving alone today since Owen was just rolling out of bed. Dawn was approaching. It was still cool with fluffy, white clouds sailing lazily across the sky.

Matt was feeling happy, contented with his life. He had settled into his California life with relative ease. Owen and Matt had grown up in the Irish community of Marine Park in New York City. Their grandparents had settled there after immigrating to the United States. Owen and Matt's father was a hard worker and joined the New York Fire Department. He supported the family well. Their mom was a dressmaker, bringing in extra income working from home. She had always been susceptible to respiratory ailments. One winter her flu bout turned into pneumonia. It was an excruciatingly sad day when they lost her. Owen was in high school at the time and Matt in junior high. Her loss turned their world upside-down.

Owen and Matt's dad seemed to lose his zest for life. His firefighting buddies had rallied around the family. Both boys went on to earn college scholarships to the business school at Columbia University. After graduation, Owen accepted the job in Santa Clarita, California.

Unfortunately, tragedy struck again. Matt's dad was killed in an accident while fighting a three-alarm fire. A flaming roof had caved in on top of him. Matt stayed on in the family home after his graduation, trying to regroup and decide in what direction to go. Then the horrific attack of 9/11 changed everything. After Matt's visit to California to see Owen, they decided to sell their dad's house in New York City. Matt moved in with Owen. They needed each other. They were family.

Arriving at the corporate offices, Matt pulled into the parking garage attached to the side of the building. It was a dark area. The dim lighting caused a shadowy effect, giving Matt an eerie feeling. As he approached the elevators, a menacing awareness crept over him. The hair on the back of his neck rose and his skin began to tingle. He heard footsteps rapidly approaching. He spun around.

"Conroy!" Matt almost shouted. "I didn't expect anyone here so early!"

"Hi, Matt. Sorry to startle you," Conroy apologized. "I have to pick up some paperwork to take to a training class on California tax law in Encino today."

Relieved, Matt said, "My department has training this morning too, learning a new software application the IT division set up for us. I'm coming in a little early to make sure everything is ready."

"Sounds great. Nice to work for a company always looking for ways to improve," stated Conroy.

They had reached the elevators when Conroy exclaimed, "I forgot my key card in my briefcase! You go ahead. I'll be right up."

Matt took the elevator up to the third floor and busied himself getting set up for the training session. His heartbeat had calmed down, but he was still a little on edge. He would put in a request for brighter lighting in the garage.

The day was so busy, Matt completely forgot about his morning scare. By the time lunchtime arrived, the training was not quite completed.

Everyone agreed to order lunch so they could finish with time left in the day to get some of their own work done. Matt called the department's secretary in and asked him to take orders and pick up sandwiches for them at the local Subway.

"Here, take my car," offered Matt, giving him the keys. "It's parked in number twelve. Don't forget the cookies and the chips!"

Matt and his training group settled back to work. The office area was quiet with most workers at the restaurant downstairs or out to lunch nearby. Without any warning, they heard what sounded like a blast. Computers jumped. The floor shook. They could hear windows shattering.

"Earthquake," someone yelled.

"That was an explosion," another exclaimed.

The evacuation alarm began screaming.

"Everyone, out," ordered Matt.

They all ran for the stairs. Before they got to the ground floor, they could already hear sirens racing to the scene.

CHAPTER NINETEEN

THE BUILDING EMPLOYEES WERE EMPTYING out into the parking lot. Faces showed shock and confusion. As others returned from lunch, they were directed to the parking lot on the other side of the street where everyone was waiting for instructions. The building adjacent to the lot had a covered area where they could wait in the cooler shade.

Matt found Owen in the crowd. Both were feeling apprehensive as to what had taken place in the parking garage. Worried, Matt asked Owen to help him search the group for his secretary, James. He must have been in the garage or should be back from Subway by now. There didn't seem to be any sign of him.

All the corporate staff had been waiting an hour so far with still no word from the police. Some frustration was understandable as the first responders were carefully evaluating the scene, setting up a command post, and placing barrier tape around the perimeter of the parking garage. Soon, two investigators came over, asking them to form a line. Once they had quieted down, one investigator asked if anyone knew who had parked his car in number twelve.

Shocked, Matt spoke up, "That's my parking spot."

"Would you please come with me," the investigator directed.

As they walked away, the other investigator began taking down everyone's name to be interviewed later. After the canines had sniffed all the cars in the garage for more explosives, they would be brought over to the group of employees to sniff any briefcases or purses. It was the heat of the day. Perspiration broke out on people's foreheads, not only from the warmth, but from anxiety and fear of the unknown. Owen walked through the group, giving reassurance that everything was going to be alright.

The manager of the building where they were corralled, wheeled out a cart of water bottles to quench their thirst. Owen nervously sipped his water, wondering what was happening with Matt. An investigator had already begun interviewing witnesses as to their relationship to the scene and where they were when it happened. Another investigator was leading a dog through the group, sniffing for signs of explosives.

In the parking garage, documents were being written describing every detail of the scene. The photographer was recording every angle. After they were done, the meticulous task of collecting evidence would begin. Everything had to be identified, labeled, collected, preserved, packaged, and transported to the various laboratories to be analyzed. It would be a long, painstaking process. Meanwhile, Matt was taken to the command tent for questioning.

"My name is Scott," the investigator introduced himself. His uniform was rumpled as if he had slept in it. He stood tall and spoke in a serious, formal manner. "Have a seat," he offered as they sat in a couple of folding chairs. "May I please have your name and your position in the company."

"My name is Matt and I work in the Human Resource Department," he responded.

"You indicated that you parked in number twelve parking space today?"

"Yes."

"Do you know who might have been by your car when it exploded?"

"It may have been our department's secretary. I sent him out to pick up lunch for us and gave him my keys so he could take my car," Matt choked turning as white as a sheet.

"We can assume then that the bomb was meant for you," Scott quietly stated. "Do you have any idea who might want to harm you?"

"I can't think of anyone."

"Where were you when the explosion took place?"

"I was on the third floor with my colleagues in a training session."

"Did you go out to your car anytime during the morning?"

"No."

"When you arrived for work this morning, did you see anyone else in the garage?"

"Yes. Conroy, from accounting, was coming in to pick up some paperwork."

"Did you speak with him?"

"Yes, briefly. Then he had to go back to his car for a key card."

"Did you see him again at any time today?"

"No."

"We are going to have to talk with you again, so we will keep in touch. Please fill out this form so we have your address and phone number."

Matt slowly walked out into the bright sunlight. His legs felt wobbly, and he felt a headache coming on. The horror of a bomb in his car was beginning to sink into his frazzled brain. And his secretary, James—killed! Were they going to think he planned to blow him up? Someone had to have planted the bomb after he got to work. It was all unfathomable!

Owen was waiting for Matt when he got back across the street. Owen looked at Matt's pale face and asked, "What happened?" He handed Matt a bottle of water.

They sat on a low wall that ran along the garden bed. Matt repeated all the questions he was asked. He explained that a bomb blew up his car probably when James, his secretary, was getting in it, going to get sandwiches.

"Do we know a good lawyer?" Matt asked. "They maybe think I planned to kill him."

Owen looked at him, the horror of the situation dawning on him. How could all this be possible? Both James and Matt were well liked. Owen could not imagine either having any enemies.

Consent-to-Search forms had been signed, so the office building was being searched for explosives. All the other cars in the garage had been searched to ensure there was not a secondary device. Investigators came over to address the waiting group. They explained that Forensics would be taking a while with their investigation. The building was cleared only to get their belongings. No one was to enter the garage until the scene had been released. Structural engineers had been called in to check for structural issues. The employees listened in stunned silence. There had been a car bomb. Someone, probably one of their staff, had been killed.

CHAPTER TWENTY

After being home from work for a couple of days, Owen and Matt were going crazy. Even endless games of pickleball could not reduce their stress level. The devastation of James' death overwhelmed them. He had been one of their group, who regularly got together at their home. His parents would be shattered at his loss.

Eric stepped out on the patio to inform Owen and Matt that he had opened the gate for a police car. Two sober looking officers explained that Matt needed to accompany them to the police station for questioning. As Matt got into the police car, Owen called their lawyer.

The interview brought out that the DNA, from body parts found at the car bombing, had identified James. The car had been rigged so that the bomb exploded when the door was opened.

Matt explained his relationship with James at work and their personal friendship. There was absolutely no reason for James' senseless death. No one else knew that James would be using his car. The conclusion was that the bomb was meant for Matt. He was to let them know if he thought of anyone who would target him. Meanwhile they would be examining all the evidence for clues.

The next day, the employees were allowed to resume work in their corporate building but still could not use the parking garage. Matt got a call from Owen part way through the day.

"Meet me for lunch at the restaurant downstairs," Owen instructed. "I have something to show you."

After picking up their food choices from the generous lunch buffet, they settled at a secluded corner table. Owen pulled an envelope out of his suit-jacket pocket and handed it to Matt.

"I found this on my desk with my mail," Owen said.

Matt unfolded the sheet of paper, seeing large, black, capital letters, "AN EYE FOR AN EYE."

"What does that mean?" Matt exclaimed with a frown.

"Revenge!"

"For what?"

"I'm not sure, yet. The only incident I can think of is our hair-raising trip from Seattle, trying to escape from Oscar and Ty!"

"What are we going to do?"

"Let's take some days off and try to figure this out," suggested Owen.

The next day, after a drawn-out morning of deliberation and brain storming, Owen said, "There's a place I want to start. I've always wondered if the drugs and weapons are still where we buried them. If they're not, what would that imply? Want to check it out?"

"Sure, let's go," Matt responded, eager to find some answers.

"Grab a couple of shovels," instructed Owen. "We're headed to Weed, near Mount Shasta."

They drove the nine hours to Weed with only a couple of short breaks. It was already dark when they arrived, so they decided to rest for the night. They would dig tomorrow and then drive back home. Owen pulled into the same motel he had stayed in with his conference group. He told the story again to Matt before they fell off to sleep.

In the morning, after a hardy breakfast, they set off to find the burial site. Owen remembered the landmark tree close to the road. It did not take long to find where they had dug. More dirt had settled in the hole from weathering, but it was still recognizable.

The blue sky was clear. The temperature was somewhere in the 80s with no hint of a breeze. They dug for a grueling hour, sweat dripping into the dry, dusty dirt. The dirt flew up as they dug, sticking to their arms and faces, turning them a dirty, tan color.

Owen stopped digging, leaning on his shovel, and exclaiming, "It's not here. Someone has taken it! There's no trace of anything, not even bullet casings."

On the drive back, they discussed the implications of how the drugs and weapons could be gone. Oscar and Ty had died in the car accident. Was it possible they had finished digging it all up before chasing them down the I-5 freeway. Maybe the drugs were burned up in the car fire. There were many questions to be answered. They needed help. Owen knew an outstanding private investigator. They would hire him as soon as they got home.

Brian met Owen and Matt at the ranch the next morning. His strong firm handshake, warmth, and self-confidence were reassuring to Matt. Brian had been a private investigator for many years, only taking personal referrals. Despite his athletic appearance, he had a common face which enabled him to easily blend into different environments. He was well known for his tenacity. He faced problems without giving up until he had an answer.

Maria served them drinks and snacks at the comfortable patio seating area while they visited. The ceiling fans were able to keep them cool as they sat in the shade, protected from the hot sun. Owen told a detailed story of the life-threatening trip they had while trying to get home after 9/11. He described everything he could remember about Oscar and Ty including sizes, voices, and tattoos.

After Owen was done, Matt recounted what had just happened at work with a car bomber targeting his car. He went through his entire day from when he got up in the morning, what he did, who he saw, who he talked to, and what questions the police had asked him.

Owen explained the note on his desk with his mail for the day, "AN EYE FOR AN EYE." Owen noted that after much reflection, he could only think of Oscar and Ty. That was the only traumatic event in his life that he could think of that would elicit a response of revenge. He told Brian about their trip to Weed and finding the drugs and weapons missing.

Armed with this detailed information, Brian assured them that he was up for this difficult challenge. He would be in touch. He requested of them that they not to talk to anyone about his investigation. Brian left them with one last word of advice, "Be ready for the unexpected!"

CHAPTER TWENTY-ONE

Conroy was reflecting on the past few days. He was swallowed up in his cozy sofa, feet up, drinking a tequila, straight. He sipped it neat, allowing himself the pleasure of tasting the subtleties of each element. He stared at his floor-to-ceiling view of the Los Angeles skyline. The golden sun was setting. Lights were beginning to twinkle across the city.

Conroy was starting to relax with the tequila taking its effect. He had received a call at his accountant training class in Encino. He was informed that there had been a car bomb explosion in his corporation's parking garage. The police had wanted to ask him a few questions.

Arriving back at work, he had checked in with the police at the command center. He had assured them that he was only there a few minutes to pick up paperwork he needed for his training class. Conroy reported not having seen anyone at that early hour except for Matt. The detective mentioned that they had yet to check the camera footage from that morning. As it turned out, they could see him and Matt by the elevators, but the camera showing Matt's car was out of order.

The day all the employees returned to work, Conroy had swung by Matt's office to express his concern. Conroy offered his support with anything he could do to help. Matt had been very appreciative. Then, Conroy had not seen Owen or Matt at work for the last few days. Maybe they would be back tomorrow. It must have been a shock to think someone tried to blow you up!

Conroy was suddenly startled by his phone ringing. Seeing it was his friend Francisco, he quickly answered. "Hola," Conroy greeted him.

After their warm and friendly greetings, Francisco said, "I've got another package for you!"

"I'll stop by after work tomorrow to pick it up. Thank you," promised Conroy.

"See you then," said Francisco.

The next day seemed to drag out forever for Conroy. It was difficult focusing on his work. He went for a brisk walk during his lunch break, trying to stay calm. He noticed that the cars that had been parked around Matt's car had been towed away as evidence. Repairs had been made. The barrier tape had been removed, and the parking garage cleaned and swept. He hoped things would get back to normal now. So far there were no suspects.

After work Conroy hurried with nervous anticipation to Francisco's warehouse. It took supreme concentration to stay within the speed limit. Just as he was parking at the back loading dock, Francisco was bringing out his package.

"Gracias!" Conroy thanked him.

"Again, Carlos wishes you good luck," relayed Francisco.

Getting safely back to his loft, Conroy secured the package in his workshop safe. Tomorrow was Friday so he would have the weekend to begin his next project. Tonight, he would sleep well.

At work the next day, Matt stopped by Conroy's office to invite him over for Saturday afternoon and evening. Matt and Owen wanted to be surrounded by their friends again, relaxing and enjoying games and good food together. Everyone had been walking on eggshells around them, not knowing what to say. Conroy was looking forward to the comradery and to seeing Maria.

Conroy worked in his workshop until he had to leave for the ranch. Everyone still seemed a little on edge. It was not long though until people were joking around, talking, and laughing, happy to be together. They played scrappy games of volleyball, and enjoyed the cool, refreshing pool. While lounging and resting, surrounded by the soothing, lush landscape, their stress seemed to melt away. Maria and Eric brought out lemon iced tea and an assortment of snacks, frozen grapes, guacamole and chips, watermelon, and quick-fueling trail mix.

Later, when the sun had slipped down behind the hills, they feasted on Eric's Italian Steak Florentine, which was complemented with sides of creamed spinach and grilled potato wedges. The sumptuous meal was topped off with Pumpkin-Gingersnap Tiramisu, served with sweet red Marsala wine.

Nobody wanted to go home, so Owen put an old movie on the giant screen in the Cabana. They reclined and drank Italian iced coffee, savoring their last hours together. While spending these hours at the ranch, Conroy felt like he had been transported to a place of enjoyment and pleasure. He helped Maria clean up, getting a little time to visit with her. Maybe one day he would be able to whisk her away to a leisure life of riches.

Most everyone had finally said their goodbyes. Owen asked Anna to stay for a while longer. They were comfy in a corner of the cabana, talking. Eric, Maria, and Matt settled in on the patio seating, recalling how wonderful it had been, being with friends again. Soon Eric headed to his apartment. Maria and Matt savored their quiet time together. Maria shared experiences from her childhood in Mexico. Matt told humorous stories of growing up in New York City. They had developed an admiration for each other and found themselves spending more and more time establishing an intimate relationship.

Arriving home, Conroy brought his thoughts back to the task at hand. He did not have much time left to prepare. His plans would be finalized in the next few weeks. Failure to carry out his long-contemplated revenge was not an option!

CHAPTER TWENTY-TWO

Owen and Matt had not yet heard a word from Brian, their private investigator. They were going about their lives as usual, trying not to get too anxious. Both could feel the weight of all their questions. The police had not come up with any answers yet either. Terrifying scenarios rattled around in their heads. At work, they parked in the lot in front of the building, despite the hot sun. They put a shade in the windshield. They were not sure if they might be targeted again.

The next day, Brian called Owen with an ominous request. He needed a DNA sample from Conroy without his knowledge. Matt noted that Conroy was often seen with a toothpick in his mouth or cleaning between his teeth with a Stim-U-Dent. He must be obsessed with having his mouth always clean and comfortable. Brian agreed that would be perfect. He would park a few blocks away from their building. Matt and Owen could collect the toothpicks from Conroy's waste basket at the end of the workday. Later, they dropped off the Stim-U-Dents they had found to Brian. There was no time to visit or ask any questions. Now they even had more possibilities keeping them awake at night.

Matt and Owen were uncomfortable having their regular group over. Instead, they just invited Anna over. Eric served Owen and Anna, and Matt and Maria, a romantic candlelit dinner with soft music playing in the background. Eric looked elegant in his black and white uniform. Instead of a jacket, he wore a black vest and had his dark, shoulder-length hair tied back in a ponytail. He genuinely enjoyed the whole process involved in creating, preparing, and serving a delectable four course meal.

Maria had decorated the table with a red linen cloth. Stunning white roses from the garden were surrounded with candles of various heights. The whole evening was magical. It seemed as if the couples' love for one another was captured and transformed into a romantic ambiance. Anna's smile dazzled from Owen's attentions. Maria's charm captivated Matt's heart. They lost track of the time and talked late into the night.

The next day, Owen, Matt, Eric, and Maria sat down together to plan for the upcoming reunion. They had decided on the long Labor Day weekend in September. This would be the second reunion of Owen's Seattle CEO conference group. When the four of them had been left to find their way home after the 9/11 attack had grounded all flights, the ensuing life-threatening trip had connected and bonded them tighter than most families. Henry and Harper were coming from Austin, Texas. Ethan, his wife, Sue, and their one-and-a-half-year-old little girl, Ava, were coming from San Jose, California. It was a healing event that they would always celebrate. This time, Owen and Matt would be proud to introduce Anna and Maria.

Eric planned the menus for the reunion. Maria instructed the housekeeping staff to prepare the bedrooms by making up the beds, providing extra pillows, setting up folding stands for suitcases, and supplying toiletries in the bathrooms along with spare towels. They also provided a basket of snacks and a basket of magazines and books near each bed. They set up a crib in Ethan, Sue, and Ava's room, along with an assortment of toys and teddy bears. The anticipation throughout the household was electrifying. It would be a weekend they would never forget.

CHAPTER TWENTY-THREE

Owen and Matt had a hard time sleeping that night. They were up before the sun. It was a perfect morning. There was a delightful gentle breeze. The pool was sparkling, inviting a cool dip later in the heat. The lawns were freshly mowed, and the irrigation system had watered the grass during the night. The lush green grass gave off a refreshing feeling. The fans on the covered patio would keep them comfortable on an eighty-degree day.

Henry and Harper arrived at the gate first. Matt and Owen waited on the grand front porch to greet them. As Henry and Harper walked toward them hand-in-hand, Matt noticed what a handsome couple they made. Henry was tall and strong, with his blond hair shining and blue eyes sparkling. Harper was confident and athletic, with caramel ribbons in her brunette hair glowing in the sunlight. Her big brown eyes were dancing with delight to be back at the ranch. After bear hugs from Owen, he and Matt grabbed suitcases and showed Henry and Harper to their suite. While they freshened up, Matt and Owen went to welcome Ethan, Sue, and Ava, who had just arrived. Ava was not quite sure how to react to the boisterous Owen, but he was great with kids, so she would quickly warm up to him. Once she was feeling comfortable in the new environment, Sue would put her down for a much-needed nap. Anna showed up next.

Owen introduced her as his "Sweetheart."

It was easy to tell by the non-stop chatter that they were all so happy to see each other. Eric and Maria settled them in at the comfortable patio table. They served a flavorful chicken salad with apples and cranberries. Ice water was served to refresh the guests after their travels. For a few moments, Owen and Matt forgot the dark cloud pressing down on them and enjoyed being surrounded by their best friends in the world.

Once Ava went down for her nap, the adults sank into the cushy patio couches and chairs, sipping on perfectly mixed mojitos. They each shared how the last year had gone for them, at work, as well as at home. Henry was still enjoying his demanding CEO job. Harper was moving up in her new company in Austin. They loved living in Henry's home. Harper had decorated it to suit their active lifestyle. Like Owen and Matt, they relished having friends over. Ethan and Sue shared a quieter life in their new, spacious condo. Ethan also was still thriving in his CEO position while Sue stayed home, taking care of Ava.

When it was Owen and Matt's turn to share, they recounted the bombing of Matt's car and the frightening aftermath. The others were shocked and horrified. They were even further disturbed to hear that the drugs and weapons were missing from where they buried them. Owen explained that they had hired a private investigator who was coming over that evening to share what he had uncovered.

Dinner that evening was a masterpiece, as always. The mood was somber, with an undercurrent of unease. Matt had a strange troubled feeling as to what Brian had discovered. By the time he arrived, Ava was down for the night.

After all the introductions were made and everyone was comfortably settled, Brian began. "I have an incredible story to tell you! To begin with, the further I got into my investigation, the more suspicious I became that Conroy was really Oscar. After getting the DNA from the Stim-U-Dents Owen and Matt provided for me, it was confirmed. Conroy is Oscar!!

I began in Seattle where you rented Oscar's repossessed car. I followed every step you all took after that, while you were being chased by Oscar and Ty. It turns out that Ty was Oscar's twin brother! Not only that, but Ty also had a life-threatening event when his kidneys failed. Oscar donated one of his kidneys to Ty and saved his life. That probably explains their very close connection to each other.

Now, when they chased you down I-5 from Weed, after digging for the drugs and weapons, they were in a rental car, rented under a false name. At the scene of the accident, when Ty was shooting at you, neither one was wearing a seatbelt. Ty was trapped in the burning car and never made it out. Oscar was thrown clear of the car, but not before experiencing severe burns to the trunk of his body, arms, and parts of his face. He managed to get away from the car, hiding under bushes in the gully. He called his drug dealing buddies, who came and picked him up. They took him to a private burn clinic to be treated. They also went back to Weed and dug up the drugs and weapons.

Once Oscar was strong enough, they moved him to a burn rehabilitation center in the Puerto Vallarta area of Mexico. There he had plastic surgery. With rhinoplasty, he had his nose reshaped. Facial implants improved his facial structure, changing his chin, cheeks, and jaw. Then, of course, you noticed his hair color change. All in all, you would not recognize him anymore as Oscar. Then he had all his rotten teeth replaced with implants. He followed a rigorous physical training program and studied accounting. With his drug cartel connections, he obtained paperwork to change his name, passport, education degrees, background, work history, and references. So, today, Oscar is now Conroy!

The police have not connected the bombing of Matt's car to Conroy, but the type of bomb is consistent with those often used by the drug cartels. With all this threatening information, I took the liberty to hire two security guards for the ranch. They will be arriving shortly. It seemed like a particularly vulnerable time with all of you here at the same time."

There was complete and utter silence when Brian finished his story. He looked around at the pale, stunned faces. Disbelief and apprehension radiated from their expressions. A chill overshadowed the group, as they all experienced an uneasy sense of foreboding. The air around them crackled with a menacing, alarming character.

The spell was broken with the arrival of the security guards. Owen met them at the gate and showed them around the grounds. Stopping at the patio, he introduced them to the reunion group, explaining that they were all staying at the ranch for the weekend. Then he and Matt showed them around the house, noting all the doors and windows. The guards recommended they all go indoors and make sure everything was locked up. They also wanted the curtains drawn and shades closed. Owen gave them a key for the cabana so they could use the bathroom, get a drink of water, or make some coffee.

Once all was secured for the night, the group gathered in the family room. No one wanted to go to bed yet. They needed to discuss what to do in this dire predicament. Brian decided to spend the night in case there were any questions. Ethan wondered if this was the right time to bring the police in on what they had discovered. Things had gotten out of hand. Leaving Conroy/Oscar out there presented a danger to them and to others. What would be the implications for them? If they did tell the police the whole story, how quickly would Conroy be arrested? Did the police have enough evidence for an arrest? There were so many questions. Brian suggested they get some sleep and discuss it further in the morning.

Everyone went to bed, but few had a restful sleep. The light from the guards' flashlights could be seen at the edges of the windows as they walked back and forth. All night they guarded the perimeter of the ranch. Occasionally, they would use their night-vision goggles to check the surrounding horse pastures, hills, and streets. All was quiet.

Matt jumped out of bed as soon as he saw the morning light. He needed his morning run. Maybe he could work off some of the stress and relieve his tension headache. He rubbed the tight muscles in his neck. An invigorating jog would help him relax, along with laps in the pool afterwards. By the time he was back, everyone would be up for breakfast, preparing for an unpredictable day, uncertain about the future.

CHAPTER TWENTY-FOUR

CONROY HAD A FITFUL NIGHT. Every detail of his long-laid plans played unendingly through his head, like a movie being shown over and over. The day before, he had rented a nondescript car under a fake name. He loaded it with some personal items and equipment. Apprehension rolled over him, but he still felt strong and confident. Nothing could go wrong.

Conroy's alarm startled him when it went off—not that he needed it. He quickly got dressed in desert camouflage from head to toe. As he drove away from his loft condo, he looked in the rear-view mirror. "Good-bye, and thanks," he sighed.

Reaching his destination, he parked at the bottom of the hill. He looked around. There were no visible lights. There were no homes on this side of the hill. Taking his precision sniper rifle out of the trunk, he slowly and quietly climbed. As he neared the top of the hill, he began to crawl, keeping his head down. Reaching the perfect spot that he had previously chosen, he slithered into the hole he had dug a few days before. In this "nest," he would wait until his prey arrived. Conroy was positioned so that he was facing straight down the road below him. He used his scopes and field glasses to prepare, did a range estimation, and set up a tripod to steady his aim. The air was very still. There was enough early light now that he could see clearly down the road to the far bend. He secured his rifle on the tripod and positioned himself squarely behind it. The recoil pad was firmly against his shoulder. His heart was beating rapidly. He took deep breaths, trying to stay calm and steady. Then he saw Matt jogging around the corner, heading down the road. Conroy was facing him, head on. He firmly held the rifle, took a deep breath, exhaled, then held his breath, and pulled the trigger. He saw Matt jerk to a stop, his hands flying to his chest as he went over backwards, landing hard on his back in the middle of the road.

Conroy grabbed his equipment and rushed down the hill. Driving to Francisco's warehouse, he changed all his clothes and shoes, left his rifle to be destroyed, and left the rental car to be thoroughly cleaned and returned. Conroy got his personal items and slid into a car driven by one of Francisco's loyal workers.

Matt was struggling to breathe! He could not seem to catch his breath. He was stunned, but conscious enough to realize he was dangerously exposed. Rolling over a couple of times, he flopped into the ditch along the side of the road. Sharp pain stabbed him in the chest, taking his breath away again. He lay perfectly still and listened. There was a roar of cars racing up the road.

The security guards had heard the shot and guessed what had happened. Two cars screeched to a stop beside Matt, the guards in one and Owen, Henry, and Ethan in the other. Matt could also hear sirens piercing the quiet morning dawn.

The guards rushed over to Matt. They didn't touch him, just looked for obvious wounds. One guard scanned the surrounding hills and pastures, looking for signs of the gunman. "Where are you hurting?" the other guard asked calmly, seeing Matt was conscious. His face was scrunched in pain.

"My chest," breathlessly responded Matt.

"You're going to be okay," the guard assured him. "The ambulance will be here shortly."

Ethan looked on in horror. "What happened?"

The guard who had been carefully checking Matt out explained, "He was shot, probably from that hill," he pointed. "He insisted on going for a run, so we fitted him with a bullet-proof vest before he left, just in case. He'll be alright."

The ambulance had pulled up. They carefully cut off Matt's vest.

"He may have some broken ribs," they surmised, "a nasty bruise, and a burn on his chest. They'll check to see if he has any internal bleeding. Lucky, he had this vest on."

The police had arrived while Matt was being gently placed on the stretcher and loaded into the ambulance. The guards and Owen stayed to explain the situation to the police. They put tape around the area of the road where Matt was shot. Others were heading up the hill to investigate where the gunman might have been.

Henry and Ethan drove back to the ranch to let the rest know what had happened. They picked up Maria. The three of them made their way to the hospital. When they arrived, Matt was having an MRI to determine if his injury had caused internal bleeding. They sat in the waiting area, somber and reflective. Maria was trying to be brave, but there were tears glistening in her eyes. Why did Matt have to go jogging this morning? Someone, likely Conroy, knew he went for a run every morning!

Owen was finally allowed to leave the shooting scene and made it to the hospital to see his brother. The doctor explained to them that he did not see any internal bleeding, but the x-rays showed three fractured ribs. He would like to keep Matt overnight and maybe for another day for observation. The physical therapist would give him breathing exercises to avoid pneumonia. He would have to ice the area and take pain medication. The healing would take about four to six weeks. The bruising and burn on his chest would take between two to four weeks to heal.

"You can see him now," offered the doctor.

"Thank you," Owen expressed gratefully.

The four of them quietly entered Matt's room. He was hooked up to an IV. His eyes were closed. He seemed to be resting comfortably. Feeling their presence, Matt opened his eyes. "Hi guys. Sorry about this," he smiled weakly.

"We're glad you're going to be okay!" exclaimed Henry. "You gave us quite a scare!"

"I know. Scared me too!" Matt agreed.

They laughed, relieving some of the tension in the room.

"Don't laugh," admonished Matt. "It hurts to even breathe."

After making sure Matt was doing well, Owen, Henry, and Ethan drove back to the ranch for a while. They needed to update the rest on what had happened and reassure them that Matt was going to be alright and home soon. Maria refused to leave Matt's side. She tenderly kissed him on the forehead and tightly held on to his hand. Matt turned his head and looked lovingly into Maria's eyes. "I love you, Maria."

"I love you too," Maria responded sincerely. "I'm glad I didn't lose you!"

"Maria, will you marry me?" he asked her.

"Yes, Matt. I will love you forever!"

Maria kissed Matt's lips, gently lingering, tears dripping onto his happy face. She held his hand through the night, while Matt got much needed, healing sleep. She would be there when he woke in the morning.

CHAPTER TWENTY-FIVE

Owen and Maria brought Matt home from the hospital at the end of the next day. He was doing well. Matt could not help but smile with Maria by his side, holding his hand. It would be fun announcing their engagement. When he was stronger, they would shop for an engagement ring and have a celebration. He looked over at her, gently squeezing her hand. Maria's face lit up. He thought it was the most beautiful face he had ever seen! Matt looked around as they drove past the gates at the ranch. He was so grateful to be alive and home. The garden flowers were colorful and lovely, and the blue sky was adorned with puffy, little clouds. The front porch was filled with all his reunion friends, waiting to welcome him home.

Everyone fussed over Matt, making sure he was comfortable. Did he need his pain medication or water to drink? Was he doing his breathing exercises? Eric was busy cooking whatever Matt chose to eat. Ava even brought him a teddy bear. Owen wanted Matt to get another good-night's sleep. Then there was serious business to discuss in the morning. Important decisions had to be made. Conroy/Oscar was not going away! When would he rear his ugly head again?

Everyone in the house had a better sleep, knowing Matt was safely back home. In the morning, after a nutritious breakfast, they got him settled in his favorite, well-used recliner. They gathered around him for a grave, critical meeting. Brian had joined them again, reporting that the police had gone to Conroy's condo. Nothing was there. It had been stripped and thoroughly cleaned. They had found his nest up on the hill from where he had shot his rifle. Investigators were working at both sites to recover any evidence they could find. The guards would remain at the ranch until Conroy was located.

Owen expressed his deep gratitude to everyone for their response to the unexpected crisis. But they were not out of the woods yet. Conroy/Oscar had gotten away! "Now, we know that AN EYE FOR AN EYE, means, A BROTHER FOR A BROTHER," expressed Owen. "Conroy is not going to give up trying to get his revenge!"

"I think I know where he is," quietly spoke Maria. "He talked a lot about Puerto Vallarta, and how much he loved it there. He said he had a place on the beach and a good friend there."

"I could go see if I can find him," offered Brian. "I have lots of connections in that area."

Maria spoke up, "I'm familiar with that area. I grew up in a village on the north side of the Bay of Banderas. It just happens that my father is the chief of police in Puerto Vallarta."

"Do you think he'd be willing to help us find Conroy?" asked Henry.

"I'm sure he would be happy to."

"I have an idea," offered Owen. "Let me know what you think. Everyone must do their part to make it work." Owen outlined his plan. Brian, Owen, Henry, and Maria would go down to Puerto Vallarta to look for Conroy with the help of Maria's father. Anna would go back to work and keep them updated on what was going on there. Ethan would oversee the ranch with Matt's limited help, while he healed. Sue and Harper would take care of Ava and Matt. Eric would stay to feed them all. Owen, Henry, Ethan, and Harper would need to take some vacation time off from their companies. The ones going to Mexico would pack and prepare today, booking a flight from Los Angeles International Airport for the next day. Ethan would drop them off.

Maria would contact her mother and father to expect them, stay at their home, and pick them up at the airport.

They all agreed on the plan and happily got busy with the preparations, relieved to have some direction. Matt rested quietly, watching and wishing he could do something to help. After the long weekend, he would contact his office. There was quite a bit of his work that he could keep up with at home. That would help pass the time while he was waiting for news from Mexico.

Early the next morning, Ethan loaded Brian, Owen, Henry, and Maria, along with their backpacks, into the largest vehicle they had at the ranch. There were hugs all around and, in some cases, long kisses. None of them wanted to leave, but it had to be done. After a fifty-minute drive, Ethan dropped them off at the airport and wished them good luck.

Arriving in Puerto Vallarta, Maria's father, Hector, picked them up in his Chevrolet Colorado police car. He drove them twenty-five miles north to the village of Bucerias. Maria's mom, Elena, and sister, Luna, warmly welcomed them to their family compound. They walked in through a garage area filled with colorful paddle boards hanging on the walls. It opened into a courtyard surrounded with a two-story home. Elena explained that she and Hector lived on one side. The kitchen and meeting room were between the living areas. Luna and her husband and baby lived on another side, and above the garage were the guest quarters. Elena and Hector invited the group to freshen up and join them for supper on the rooftop terrace. It was beautifully furnished with wicker couches and soft cushions and a dining table with wicker chairs. The terrace had a BBQ section and looked out over the marina and blue waters of the bay. A thatched roof provided them needed shade.

Elena and Luna served tacos dorados, deep fried with chicken breast. Choices to drink were soda and beer. Coffee was served with dessert—marbled três leches cake, made with condensed evaporated milk and full cream. There was not a crumb left on anyone's plate.

When Elena and Luna left to clean up, Owen, Henry, Brian, and Maria relaxed with Hector, telling him the whole sordid story of Conroy/Oscar from beginning to end. They organized a plan to begin searching the next day. Brain and Maria spoke Spanish, so they would team up with the other two. Brian and Henry would begin in the marina area, and Owen and Maria on the El Malecon, boardwalk along the waterfront. They would be going shop to shop, showing Conroy's picture. Maybe someone would recognize him.

They kept in close touch with the ranch, letting them know their plans. Maria was staying in a room in her parents' quarters, getting to bed late after catching up with the family news. The next day was going to be challenging for them all.

CHAPTER TWENTY-SIX

The next morning, Maria and her guests were up early, anxiously getting ready for the day. Elena served up a hearty breakfast of tasty Huevos Rancheros—fried eggs, Mexican style— fried corn tortillas smothered in cooked salsa, and strong coffee.

The weather was hot and humid. Heavy, storm clouds laced with lightning hung above the bay. It was the rainy season. The guys dressed in lite T-shirts and Maria in a tank top. Hector gave them each a rain poncho to add to their backpack supplies of water, snacks, phones, and pictures of Conroy. When they were ready, they thanked Elena for breakfast and were on their way to Puerto Vallarta. Hector dropped Brian and Henry off first at the marina, then Owen and Maria at the north end of the El Malecon.

The teams went shop to shop, business to business, showing people Conroy's picture, and asking if they had seen him or knew him. Hector was alerting his police force also, so that they could begin inquires around the city.

Owen and Maria were getting tired and discouraged by the time they got to the last few shops on the waterfront. They were almost to the river Cuale. Greeting a shopkeeper, they repeated their explanation and showed him the picture.

"Si, I know him. That is Senores Conroy, but I have not seen him for a long time. He would jog down the boardwalk and back every day," explained the shopkeeper.

"Do you know where he lived?" questioned Maria.

"No, but he would always run across the bridge over the river. He must live in that area of town."

"Do you remember when you last saw Conroy?" Owen inquired.

"No. It has been months, I think."

"Gracias," Maria thanked him.

It was time to meet Hector at the corner where he was picking them up. Next, they rendezvoused with Henry and Brian. On the drive back to Bucerias, Owen shared what the shopkeeper had told them. Everyone was pleased and excited with the progress they had made in one day. Hector suggested they all work on the other side of the river the next morning.

Getting back to the family compound, Maria proposed they change out of their sweat-soaked clothes. She would take them down to the beach. Luna joined them as they carried their paddle boards the few blocks to the seaside. The clouds had dumped their load of torrential rain. The sun shimmered on the blue water, outlined with miles of white sand. Restaurants and bars spilled out onto the sand with chairs and tables by the edge of the waves. They stood in awe, taking in the beautiful sights.

Soon they were all on their boards, enjoying the warm, tropical water of the bay. This was exactly what they needed to unwind after a stressful day. Lying down on their colorful towels on the hot sand, they talked about their homes and families. They shared with Luna what information they had found out from the shopkeeper.

Later, after another delicious meal, the four met with Hector to form a strategy for the next day. The atmosphere was charged with anticipation. Two of them would follow along the beach. The other two would start at the river, going up and down the streets that ran down to the beach. If anyone got a lead, they would call Hector, who would come and pick them up. After checking how Anna, Matt, and the others at the ranch back home were doing, the four had a restful night of sleep. Anna reported that things at work were going smoothly. Matt was healing and walking around more. They all missed them and sent their love.

In the morning, the four were eager to continue their search for Conroy. This time, Brian and Henry followed the pathway along the beach and Owen and Maria went along the streets perpendicular to the beaches. There was a stiff breeze blowing off the water, which made them feel a little cooler. Along the beach, Brian and Henry stopped at every thatched-roof palapa, showing people Conroy's picture. In front of a beautiful and luxurious condo building, they encountered a soaking wet couple relaxing with their drinks. Brian introduced Henry and himself, explaining for whom they were looking. Senores Sergio looked up from the picture.

"That's Conroy, my neighbor. He lives on the fourth floor," Sergio informed them, pointing up to Conroy's balcony.

Henry and Brian stood stunned and shocked until Brian finally found his voice, "Have you seen him recently?"

"Yes, I hadn't seen him for a few months, so I was surprised to see him yesterday. He was only here a short time. It seemed like he was just picking up some clothes," observed Sergio.

"Do you know where he went?" asked Henry.

"No, but you could ask Rosa at the bar inside. She might know better than I do."

They thanked Sergio and went around to the bar. They saw Owen and Maria working their way down the street and signaled them to come over. Joining up, they told them what Sergio had said. Owen and Maria were elated. They headed over to the bar to see if Rosa was at work. She recognized Conroy immediately. She knew that he would make trips up into the mountains to stay with a friend, but she did not know where. They thanked her and called Hector with the news.

Hector took them to the police headquarters, a building with more coastal architecture and open arches which let in the ocean breezes. They sat in a comfortable conference room with a ceiling fan cooling them. They were served ice water and made to feel welcome. Hector and a couple of his detectives sat down around the expansive table with the group. They reported to the police officers what they had found out about Conroy in the last two days. He had been seen yesterday, but was not staying in his condo. The detectives were drone surveillance experts and would search the mountains for where Conroy might be staying. Their informants had given them some direction as to the identity of this friend of Conroy's. They suspected he had contacts with the local drug cartel. It was up to them now to find him. They would keep Hector updated on their progress.

CHAPTER TWENTY-SEVEN

Owen, Henry, Brian, and Maria were gathered on the rooftop terrace at Maria's family compound. The tension of insomnia showed on their faces, along with their feelings of frustration and helplessness. Waiting for news was exhausting. The police had used their drones to find Carlos' hideout in the Sierra Madre mountains above the city of Puerto Vallarta. They were keeping it under surveillance, as well as Conroy's condo on the beach. The police also came to an agreement with Senores Sergio. When he was told the situation, he promised to call Hector immediately if he sighted Conroy at the condo building.

It grew hotter as the day dragged on. The group of four sensed the beach calling out to them. They needed the cooling of the ocean. The distractions of the coastline, busy restaurants, and sand between their toes were essential to their wellbeing. They sipped Pina Coladas while the waves crept closer to their beach chairs. The palm trees were swaying in the windy afternoon as they relaxed in the salty spray. For a few moments, they felt carefree and lazy in their seaside paradise. Another rainstorm was brewing in the far distance across the bay, threatening to end their peacefulness. They saw this as an omen. A feeling of foreboding settled over them as they made their way back to the compound. Where was Conroy? What was he doing?

At dawn of the next day, Hector received a call from his lookouts. They had spotted a Jeep Wrangler a block away from Conroy's building. Senores Sergio had seen him walking down the sidewalk and then Conroy entered the building. Hector's police force was planned and prepared. They jumped in their vehicles, ready to follow Conroy once he came back out. It was about an hour before he reappeared. Coming out the main entrance door, he hesitated, looking up and down the street cautiously before venturing out to his car. After a quick stop for supplies, Conroy sped into the safe cover of the mountain jungle.

The sky was darkening. Thick, gigantic, ominous clouds were rolling in overhead. Suddenly, there was a chill in the air as wind swirled through the trees. Conroy swerved as palm fronds whipped across the road. Huge splashes of water began to pelt the windshield. He could hear the thunderstorm racing above the trees. Bright, flashing lightning lit up the sky like fireworks.

The chase was on. Conroy could see the speeding police cars closing in on him. Banging, crashing thunder roared furiously, seemingly making his jeep shudder. His chest was pounding. Lightning was sizzling, zipping across the sky. Conroy accelerated around the corner and onto the turnoff to Carlos' place, powering his jeep through the oozy mud. The next obstacle would be the swiftly moving, swollen river ahead. Since the last hurricane had taken out the bridge, Carlos had built a temporary pedestrian rope bridge for the rainy season, when it was impossible to drive across.

The all-terrain mud tires on the police vehicles were providing superb traction on this tough, mucky road. They were close behind Conroy's jeep. The landscape became marshy as they approached the river.

Hearing the roar of the crashing river, Conroy slammed on the brakes, causing the jeep to slide in the mud. Flinging open his door, he sprang out, racing for the rope bridge. Gripping the side support ropes, he stepped out onto the first slippery slat of wood. Behind him, he could hear the loud rumble of the car engines as they rapidly approached the bridge, like large jungle cats ready to pounce on their prey. As Conroy stretched to find the next slat of wood, he could also hear the driving rain, which sounded like the buzzing of angry bees. The slats were far apart and slick from the rain and the frothing spray of the river.

Clinging on to the ropes for his life, he took a couple more steps. He knew he had to move faster. Suddenly, as he reached out his leg for the next step, lightning slashed the sky with blinding shards of light. His foot hit the edge of the slat and he slipped. He clamored helplessly, trying to get a secure hold on the slimy ropes. The unstable bridge swayed. Conroy lost his grip, slipping between the slats, and splashing into the dark, raging water below. The river swept Conroy around a bend, and he plummeted over a waterfall into a calmer pool, where hungry crocodiles patiently waited.

The police were able to collect a few human remains that were thrown up onto the banks. Those would provide them with positive identification. There was no denying that Conroy had met his fate. Every decision he had made led him to this alarming demise.

Owen, Henry, Brian, and Maria waited late into the stormy night for Hector to return home. Around the cozy fireplace in the family meeting room, Hector told them the whole story. He recalled spotting Conroy as he came out of his condo building, following him, and chasing him up the mountain. Hector described the rope bridge and Conroy's plunge into the river. Lastly, Hector related the dreadful scene of the crocodiles' violent feeding frenzy. He assured the group that their lab would be able to identify Conroy from the remains found on the banks.

It was a shocking, unbelievable ending to Conroy's/Oscar's and Ty's story. Unwittingly, the Seattle conference group had been pulled, as unsuspecting characters, into the terrifying plot.

In life, there are positive and negative connections. Positive connections to people are supposed to lower our levels of anxiety and depression. They help us develop greater empathy for others, which makes us more open to trusting. Social connections should help us regulate our emotions and should lead to higher self-esteem. These connections should increase our happiness, afford us better health, and extend our lives.

The reality is that we often find ourselves living in a world of true disconnection.

CHAPTER TWENTY-EIGHT

Owen, Brian, Henry, and Maria each received a hero's welcome as they returned to the ranch in Santa Clarita. There were hugs, kisses, slaps on the back, high-fives, fist pumps, laughter, and joyful chatter. The dark, threatening cloud that had been hanging over them had dissipated. The ranch was back to a place of peacefulness and safety.

That evening, as a thank you to Maria and her family, Eric served his mouthwatering enchiladas. His tangy Mexican slaw was a perfect complement to the rich, cheesy entrée. Maria's favorite side was the Mexican street corn—grilled to perfection, slathered in a creamy sauce, and sprinkled with cheese.

There was a close feeling of connection around the table as they shared the meal. They all felt a sense of trust and cooperation. It was a time of comfort, celebration, and love. Best of all, there was a deep, shared feeling of gratitude for life.

Later in the evening, everyone gathered on the patio to share the events that happened while they were separated. Of course, the big story was all the details of how Conroy was tracked down and how he lost his life. A huge part of the story was about Maria's amazing family and the part they played. A deep bond had been formed with her family—an authentic connection.

They had all worked together to solve a life-threatening problem. The families would certainly be spending wonderful times together in the future.

Those who had stayed back on the ranch had also formed a new depth of connection and friendship. Eric and Ethan had made sure everything on the ranch was running smoothly. It was a great comfort to Sue knowing that Ethan was not in the path of danger again. Ava was a fun source of entertainment and laughter, keeping the tension at bay. Harper cared for Matt, keeping him comfortable and on a healing routine. Anna checked in every day and brought Matt's work from his human resource department at the office. They pulled together as a team, supporting each other through uncertain, tragic circumstances.

Now it was time to party! Eric, Ethan, Sue, Harper, and Anna had planned a party for the next day. Anna had invited their friends from work. By seven o'clock in the evening, everyone had arrived, happy to see each other again. The house was filled with flickering candles, creating an intimate atmosphere. Small bouquets of lively, colorful flowers were placed throughout the rooms. Maria, her thick dark curls swept back from her forehead, led people to the loaded buffet table. Anna, her face radiant in the flickering candlelight, gracefully assisted her. Eric had worked all day preparing a delectable buffet. For entrees, he had roasted a juicy, flavorful pork loin and prepared chicken empanadas with flaky, buttery crusts. Huge plates of appetizing sides accompanied the meal—potato skins, croquettes, and perfect, fluffy, savory, sweet corn fritters. In addition, they served a colorful salad with "choose-your-own" ingredients. The platter contained five rows of fresh vegetables, loads of fresh greens, and grated cheddar and mozzarella cheeses. A homemade vinaigrette dressing topped it off. Anna had added her contribution, deviled eggs, which were insanely creamy and packed with flavor. Each person had their own little bottle of Rosè wine. Eric, as usual, had outdone himself with his skills and labor of love.

When a little time had elapsed to allow the exquisite meal to settle, the house filled with lively, joyous dance music. Everyone could not help but feel the rhythms taking over their bodies. The ping pong table and furniture had been moved to make room for a dance floor. Soon it was filled with the beauty and energy of dancers expressing joy and happiness, as they relaxed and had fun.

Suddenly, the music stopped. The dancers came to a halt, looking over at Owen, who was standing with his arm around Anna. Matt slowly stood and held Maria's hand as they joined them.

"We have a surprise for you," Owen announced. "I asked Anna to marry me, and she said YES!"

Everyone cheered and clapped, while smiling, laughing, and congratulating them.

"I have an announcement, too," spoke Matt. "When I was in the hospital bed, I asked Maria to marry me, and she said YES!"

That brought the house down with hearty cheers. Eric brought out trays of champagne. They toasted the two engagements. Dreamy dance music floated throughout the celebration. Everyone watched the two couples slow dance. Then they all joined in.

Afterwards, Eric served mini cheesecakes with rich fillings and crunchy graham cracker and pecan crusts, along with more champagne.

The mesmerizing beat of the music drew them all together again, swaying and twirling on the dance floor. With the promise of tomorrow, they danced the night away.